C000215582

Exe Ray Vision

Lockwood and Darrow
Book 4

Suzy Bussell

Exe Ray Vision

Lockwood and Darrow Book 4

By Suzy Bussell

This is a work of fiction. All of the characters, organisations, and events portrayed in this novel are either products of the author's imagination or are used fictitiously.

Copyright © 2022 by Suzy Bussell.

All rights reserved.

The moral right of Suzy Bussell to be identified as the author of this work has been asserted by her in accordance with the Copyright, Designs and Patents Act, 1988.

Ebook ISBN: 978-1-915717-01-6

Paperback ISBN: 978-1-915717-02-3

No part of this book may be used or reproduced in any manner whatsoever without the prior written permission of the author. eBooks are not transferable. They cannot be sold, shared or given away as it is an infringement on the copyright of this work.

Chapter One

Angus Darrow and Charlotte Lockwood, Devon Private Detectives stood outside the Devon County rugby stadium in the south of Exeter city.

Built seven years ago, the club had gone from strength to strength, and so had the amount of fans that followed them. Now, during the rugby season, home games meant a flood of fans, both local and away-visitors. A few years ago, when the team had entered the Premiership League, its future had been assured as one of the best clubs in the country.

Angus had driven them across Exeter and parked his black VW Golf in one of the visitors' spaces near the entrance.

"You know, I've driven past this place countless times in the last few years, but I've never been here." Charlotte looked up at the Devon County Rugby Club logo: a rugby ball held by two large hairy hands, with the green, white and black Devon flag in the background.

"I've been to a few matches over the years." Angus adjusted his red tie. He was wearing a navy-blue three-piece suit and a white shirt. The red tie gave a nice splash of colour and Charlotte liked the waistcoat: it suited him. She gave him a quizzical look. "I didn't have you down as a rugby fan."

Angus pushed his glasses up his nose. "There's lots you still don't know about me."

"Clearly." Charlotte narrowed her eyes. "Let me guess: you came here when you were in the police doing crowd control."

"Guilty as charged," Angus responded, with a chuckle. "Although I didn't get to watch the matches – too busy."

"I still haven't seen a photo of you in uniform," Charlotte complained.

His face broke into a smile. "It's been a long time since I was in uniform, even before I left the police."

"I bet you looked very dashing." She smiled, imagining what he had looked like.

"I was very glad to become a detective and wear my own clothes. Though with a uniform, I didn't have to think about what to wear."

She looked him up and down. "Yes. Should it be the blue suit ... or the dark-blue suit..."

"Ha ha," he said drily. "You have no idea how hard it is to pick."

"Let me see... If you joined the police when you were in your twenties—"

"Late twenties."

"Late twenties, that was before smartphones. So hacking your phone for a photo wouldn't work. I wouldn't go through your belongings. Hmm, maybe my brother has a photo of you." Mark 'Woody' Lockwood was still in the police and had worked with Angus back in the day. Charlotte made a mental note to ask when she next spoke to him.

"Shall we go in?" asked Angus.

Charlotte grinned. "Nice change of subject there. Good move."

They approached the main entrance and went through the huge glass doors. The receptionist sitting behind the front desk was in her mid-twenties, dressed in a smart white blouse and wearing a lanyard around her neck with photo ID badge. She looked up from typing. "Hello, can I help?"

"Angus Darrow and Charlotte Lockwood to see Mr Trevor Holland," Angus said.

She looked at the computer screen, clicked the mouse, then looked up and smiled. "If you would like to wait over there, I'll let him know you've arrived."

They went over to the waiting area, which had two office-style settees and a low coffee table. They sat down next to each other and took in the entrance area. On all the walls were photos of rugby players in action, each one carefully selected to show each man immersed in the game.

Charlotte winced and stretched her leg. She'd broken it during their last case and the plaster cast had only come off six weeks ago.

"Is it still hurting?" Angus nodded at her leg, encased in smart black jeans.

She sighed. "A little. The physiotherapy has been pretty intense. I didn't think it would take so long to get back to normal."

"Why haven't you ever been here before?" he asked changing the subject.

Charlotte wrinkled her nose. "Rugby's not really my thing. Or football. Or any other sport, actually. Idris was always a big fan, though. Supports Cardiff."

"So you must know a lot about rugby, then?"

"Not at all. We always had our own interests, and that

was one of his. He'd take Gethin and Rhys at least once a month. I didn't mind: it gave me time to myself to go to the spa." Charlotte examined the club logo on display in several places around the reception area: "What are the huge hairy hands about?"

"It's from the Dartmoor legend."

"I've not heard of it."

"Really? According to the legend there's a road near Postbridge where a pair of dismembered hairy hands appear from nowhere, grab the steering wheel of the car, or whatever vehicle you're driving and force you off the road. There were lots of reported accidents about a hundred years ago."

Charlotte gave a little shiver. "That's horrible. Why would they put something like that in their logo?"

"It's not real. One of the many legends of Dartmoor to keep the tourists interested. The investigations into the accidents found that stretch of road had a bad camber. They fixed it, and the accidents stopped."

"I suppose the hairy hands make a good gimmick in the matches for the crowds to wear. Is that why there are comedy pairs for sale?" Charlotte indicated to a glass display case which had a variety of club merchandise: hats, scarfs, mugs, t-shirts and gloves with hair on the back.

The lift doors opened and a white-haired man in his sixties, wearing a mid-blue waistcoat and matching trousers stepped out. "Mr Darrow?"

Angus stood up and they shook hands. "Trevor Holland," he said.

"This is my colleague, Charlotte Lockwood." Angus indicated her, and she stood up.

"Pleased to meet you," said Trevor. "My office is on the second floor, if you'd like to follow me?"

They followed him into the lift. Thirty seconds later,

they were shown into a large, bright office overlooking the car park at the front. "Can I offer you a coffee or tea?" Trevor asked.

Charlotte wanted to say yes, but she caught Angus's eye and shook her head. Drinks from strangers were definitely off the menu, after the time when a suspect had tried to drug them both with a coffee.

"Not at the moment," Angus replied.

Despite being in a modern, fresh building, Trevor's office had an antique feel about it. There was a huge dark wood desk with a computer and an executive chair. In the corner near the window was a grandfather clock and there were several landscape paintings with ornate frames. Instead of seating himself at his desk and offering them the chairs opposite, Trevor indicated an area behind them with three tub chairs and a coffee table. They each took a seat.

"How can we help you, Mr Holland?" Angus took out his notepad and pen.

Trevor flexed his shoulders. "Call me Trevor. We have a very delicate matter that needs looking into, and I must be assured of your utmost discretion."

Angus's pen was poised above the notepad. "We're happy to sign a non-disclosure agreement."

"An NDA won't be necessary at this stage, but thank you. You come highly recommended."

"Who by?"

"Thomas Lambert."

Charlotte and Angus shared a brief glance. Tom had asked Angus to look into the disappearance of a vulnerable teen a while ago. It had been Charlotte and Angus's first case together.

"Our reputation depends on us being discreet at all

times," Angus stated. "We would never disclose anything a client tells us without permission."

"Very well. In that case, we've been receiving some nasty messages through our social media platforms." Trevor held up a hand. "I know what you're about to say – that's not unusual. Anyone with a public profile gets them all the time. It's particularly bad with sports clubs. If we lose, we get hate not only from the fans but the opposition. If we win, we still get it. Sometimes from the fans, too."

"But these are different?" Angus asked.

Trevor shifted in his seat. "Yes. They started off just like the normal troll posts, but over time they've been getting nastier and nastier. Our social-media manager blocked the offending accounts, but they keep finding ways of getting round that."

Charlotte sat up. "How do you know it's the same person?"

"They have continuity, and they reference things only that person would know they said before. It's quite sinister."

"They usually are," Charlotte replied. "But often it's teenagers, and their parents have no idea what they're up to."

"I hope that's the case. Anyway, we need you to find out who's behind the messages so that we can make them stop. We have our lawyers poised to act as soon as you've rooted them out. They've said we can take whoever's behind this to court for stalking and defamation." Trevor leaned forwards. "You see, they're accusing some of the players of match-fixing. It's not so unusual: some fans accuse other clubs all the time. But this is persistent and they're claiming they have proof."

"That is bad," Charlotte commented.

Trevor turned to her. "It is, and they won't stop. Of

course, they're referencing Michael Beech. He was investigated by his previous club for match-fixing, something he always denied, and he was exonerated. This is why we think it's someone who knows him. Only a few people know about the investigation at his previous club. It was kept very quiet because no one wanted it to get out. Stories like that can ruin clubs and players."

"And there was no evidence of match-fixing from him?" Angus asked.

"Absolutely not. We wouldn't have taken him on if there was an inkling of doubt."

"But you knew about it?" said Charlotte.

"Michael was honest with us. When we were in discussions with him about a transfer, he brought it up. He wanted us to know so that if it came up in the future, it wouldn't be a surprise. He's an amazing young man." Trevor's expression became animated. "He came from very humble beginnings and has worked his way up to be one of the best players in the country. Lots of people, unfortunately, don't want working-class men like him making a success of themselves. Rugby is still seen as a sport for private schools and the middle class."

"Do you think that might be the motivation behind the threats?" Angus asked.

Trevor shrugged. "It's a possibility. That's what I'm hoping you'll find out."

Charlotte blinked twice. "There's every chance the person or people behind it won't be in the UK."

"We have evidence that they're here in Exeter. From some of the things they've said, we think they know some of the players personally. "

Angus started writing in his notebook. "Charlotte is a

cyber expert. She'll be able to find out as much as is humanly possible about who's behind this."

Charlotte smiled at Angus's praise. "I'll need to speak to your social-media manager, possibly the network manager, and anyone else who's dealt with the messages. I'll need certain information from the messages to trace them."

"Of course," Trevor replied. "I'll take you to our computer department, who will give you access to everything you need. I'm terrible with technology, so I'll leave you to iron out the details."

Trevor stood up and they followed him a short distance down the corridor to another office. It also overlooked the car park, but it was smaller and dingier, with lower-grade furniture, a smaller window and six desks packed into the space.

Charlotte sighed to herself. The techies always got the worst treatment in companies, even though their job was often the most important. At least at a rugby club their job *was* second to the players and coaches, but it still annoyed her.

One of the desks was empty, and the others were occupied by men in their late twenties or early thirties, at a push. All were dressed in jeans and T-shirts with scruffy hair.

"This is our tech department," Trevor said as they entered. "The beating heart of all things computing. I'm not sure what they all do, but they keep everything running ship-shape. Usually."

None of the techies looked up. An oversized man sat at the middle desk, with long hair in a pony-tail and a T-shirt that said *No. I won't fix your computer,* selected a crisp from a large packet and crunched on it.

"Daniel over there is our head of social media." Trevor pointed to a man of about thirty, with dark-brown hair and matching beard, dressed in a plain t-shirt. "Daniel, this is Mr Darrow and Ms Lockwood. They're here about *that* issue."

Daniel stood up and smiled. "Hi."

Charlotte stepped forward. "Let's talk things over, then I'll see what I can find."

Daniel brought chairs and Angus and Charlotte joined him in front of the computer. His desk was uncluttered, containing just his monitor, a half-drunk mug of coffee and an empty notepad.

"I'll leave you to it," Trevor said, from the door.

"Can you start from the beginning?" asked Charlotte. "When did the first message arrive?"

"It was a few weeks ago." Daniel typed on the keyboard and opened a document. "I've been logging it all here." It was a word processor document listing screenshots and messages. There were pages of it.

He clicked the mouse and the start of the document appeared. "It started four weeks ago. The first messages were emails." He scrolled down. "When those were ignored, he started using Twitter, Instagram and TikTok private messaging." He scrolled again to show further screenshots of threatening messages.

The match fixing is obvious. Everyone knows.

The players make it so clear. Dropping the ball, fumbling with it. Which players aren't throwing the game?

I watched the game Saturday and it was obvious players threw it.

Then a week later:

Match fixers! You utter scum, I'm going to go to the press to expose your fixing. The world needs to know what your up to.

And

The fans need to know your fixing matches. I will expose you. You utter bastards.

Charlotte winced at the incorrect 'your' instead of 'you're'. She felt that if anyone was going to write nasty messages over the internet, they could at least get the grammar correct.

There was more messages except they got longer and more explicit about which websites, newspapers and self-professed conspiracy theorists on YouTube they would go to with evidence and they named the players with clips from matches apparently showing proof of them purposefully throwing the game.

"I'll need the original emails to trace who sent them," said Charlotte.

"We've tried that already. The IP address was sent through a VPN."

Charlotte narrowed her eyes, a reaction Angus recognised. She was trying to contain her dislike of the man and clearly a VPN, wouldn't to stand in her way. She managed to smile at Daniel. "I'd still like them, anyway."

Daniel nodded. Charlotte handed him a USB flash drive, which he plugged into the computer, then sent the files to download.

"Do you always log nasty messages?" she asked.

"Only the really nasty ones. However, I've noticed that a lot of them start off with a small dig and then get worse. We had a really bad troll a few years ago. It stopped after about six months. These people on the internet, they think they have the right to have a go at everyone. And most people care, and get upset, you see." He sat back. "If there's anything else you need, just ask. Mr Holland told me to give you any help I can."

"Thank you."

Chapter Two

They left not long afterwards, reassuring Trevor that they would start on the case straight away. Charlotte paused by the car. "I'm sure I can find information about who's behind the messages. Shall we go back to your house?"

"Don't you need your computer?"

"No, I can log into it remotely using my tablet."

They got into the car and set off. But when Angus turned left into a side road near his house, in front of him was a line of four cars. Ahead of those, a police car was parked beside a blue road sign that said "*POLICE INCIDENT: ROAD CLOSED*"

One by one, the other drivers turned their cars around and drove off. When Angus reached the front, he stopped the car and got out.

"What's going on?" Angus asked the police officer in the car, whom he didn't recognise.

"The road will be shut for a few days. World War 2 bomb found in the back garden of one of the houses."

Angus's eyebrows shot up. "A bomb?"

"Yeah, I know." The officer grinned. "Buried in the garden all these years without going off. Not sure what they'll do about it yet, but obviously it needs sorting." The officer spoke in a patronising tone that Angus didn't like. "Do you live near here, sir?"

"Yes." Angus told him his address.

The officer sucked in his breath. "That's just a few houses from where the bomb is. They're evacuating everyone within a half-mile radius until bomb disposal come and deal with it."

"OK, but I need to get to my house."

"They haven't decided when you'll be allowed back yet but you'll need to find alternative accommodation until bomb disposal have finished."

"When can I go in?"

"Not sure yet. You'll have to bear with us. We don't want anyone getting hurt."

Angus winced. He had washing in the machine that would have finished by now, and all he had was the clothes he was standing in.

The officer saw his expression. "I understand that it's frustrating, sir, but we must let the bomb-disposal team do their work. If you give me your details, we can contact you to keep you up to date."

Angus wrote them down, then got back into the car.

Charlotte raised her eyebrows. "Is everything all right?"

"Not really." Angus explained about the bomb and the exclusion zone.

"A World War 2 bomb near your house, and it's been there all those years?" Charlotte snorted. "It won't go off unless they touch it."

"I know. But they've cordoned it off, so there's nothing I can do."

"So you can't even pick up some stuff? What if you had a pet?"

"I don't, though."

"You could tell them you do. It's not like they'd follow you to check, is it?"

Angus gave a small shake of his head. "I won't lie."

"You're such a stickler for the truth."

He started the engine. "Most of the time. Not always."

"Go on, then, tell me a time when you've lied." Charlotte grinned and waited.

Angus looked out through the windscreen and thought hard, but nothing came. He didn't like lying, and he didn't do it.

He sighed. "All right, I can't think of any."

"I knew it." Charlotte said smugly. "Some people are pathological liars, but you, you're ... a pathological truth-teller."

Angus pushed his glasses up his nose. She was right, of course. "I'd rather not say anything than tell a lie."

"It's not a bad thing, Angus. Some people lie all the time, and it causes havoc in their lives. Anyway, you can stay at my house for as long as you need to. I've got plenty of spare rooms. You can pick the one you like best."

"Thanks, but hopefully it won't come to that, and I'll get home tonight."

He turned the car round and headed for Charlotte's house in Topsham, his mind whirling with dismal possibilities. He wondered if his house insurance would cover any damage. Then he imagined his house left an uninhabitable shell if the bomb exploded. Then he managed to pull himself up short. *It's never any use thinking about what could go wrong. Be prepared, but don't worry about what hasn't happened yet.*

He glanced at Charlotte, who was watching him. "Do you think they'll do a controlled explosion, or defuse it onsite?"

He huffed out a breath. "I hope they'll defuse it. It's too close to the houses to do a controlled explosion, surely?"

Charlotte was looking out of the window. "I suppose so. They found a bomb on the beach in Sidmouth not so long ago and did a controlled explosion. I saw footage of it on the internet. But I suppose it was less risky doing that there because it wasn't near anything."

Back at Charlotte's, they went into the kitchen. Charlotte sat down at the breakfast bar and massaged her calf with her hand, wincing.

"Should that still be hurting? That's the second time today you've been rubbing it." Angus put his hands in his pockets.

She glanced up at him. "It sort of tingles and it doesn't feel right. The doc keeps telling me to be patient and that it will get better eventually. Apparently, it's perfectly normal. I've been taking over-the-counter painkillers, but I'm trying to stay off them if possible."

"You stay there and I'll make you a cup of tea."

"Thanks."

Angus opened a deep drawer under the espresso machine and took out two mugs. One had the slogan: *I like my coffee #000000*, and the other: *I only need coffee on days ending with a Y*.

He held up the first mug. "I keep meaning to ask – what's the joke?"

Charlotte smiled. "It's a programmer in-joke - #000000 is the computer code to display black."

Angus sighed. "I might have guessed it would be something to do with computers." Then he looked around. "Where's your kettle?"

"Oh, I don't have one now. I've had the tap changed to one that can instantly heat the water to boiling point." She pointed to the sink. "Try it, it's really good. Just press the red button then turn it on, and voila, boiling water straight away."

Angus eyed the tap cautiously. Instant hot water might be a good idea but there was something therapeutic about waiting for the kettle to boil. It gave you time to think.

He pressed the button and out came boiling water. Charlotte watched him as she massaged her leg. "If you press the blue button it does cold filtered water, and if you press the green button it makes it fizzy."

Angus rolled his eyes as he squeezed the teabags in the mugs. "Does it mix cocktails, too? Wine on tap? Beer?"

"Haha. Although I'd buy one that made mojitos."

"I thought you weren't drinking."

"Most of the time. I lapsed on holiday."

"Understandable." He handed her the mug of tea and she took a sip.

Angus sat down beside her at the breakfast bar. "What's the first step, then? Are you clear on what you need to do to hunt this person down?"

"Of course." Charlotte took another sip of tea. "Hunt them down is the right term, too," she said, with a smirk.

If she had been anyone else, Angus would have thought them completely arrogant. But Charlotte had good reason to be certain. She was brilliant, and Angus had learnt to appreciate that she knew she was, too.

"I could tell you what I'm going to do to track them down," she added, "but your eyes would just glaze over."

"That's true. I'll leave you to it, and get on with

answering emails and WhatsApp messages." He moved to the other side of the room and took out his phone.

He was deep in answering emails half an hour later when his phone rang. The caller ID showed a number with a local code. He answered it straightaway. "Hello?"

"Mr Angus Darrow?" said a female voice.

"Yes."

"I'm from the council. I've been assigned to give updates to all residents affected by the WW2 bomb." She paused as if waiting for him to respond. "The latest news is that the bomb is too large and dangerous to move, so the bomb disposal team will have to do a controlled explosion. That will take a few days to prepare, because they have to bring in a great deal of sand to make sure it explodes into the air."

This was starting to sound complicated.

"So we are asking for everyone within a half-mile radius to evacuate the area until it's all over – and obviously that includes you. Do you have somebody that you could stay with till then?"

Angus's mind ran through people he knew. Tom? Possibly. Malcolm was on holiday in Spain. Maybe James. Rhona? No: he'd rather stay in a hotel.

And of course there was Charlotte. He looked over at her typing away, completely immersed in what she was doing. She'd already offered for him to stay.

"Are you still there?" asked the council worker.

"Er, yes. Yes, I am." Angus ran a finger round the inside of his collar.

"If you can't find somewhere, the council will provide accommodation, but that will be the holiday camp in Exmouth. We haven't been able to find anything else at such short notice as all the hotels are fully booked."

"I'll find somewhere." Angus sighed. "Can I at least go and get some clothes and other belongings?"

"Yes, provided you're quick. And make sure you tell the police at the road block what you're doing. We aren't expecting the bomb to explode after all this time, but for everyone's safety, we'd prefer that people stay away as much as possible. Can I add you to a WhatsApp group for further updates? That will save more phone calls."

"Yes, sure. Thanks." Angus ended the call.

Charlotte looked up. "Was that news about the bomb?" She carried on typing.

He put his phone down and rubbed his temples. "They're going to do a controlled explosion in a few days' time. In the meantime, I have to stay away."

She smiled. "I have plenty of room: you can stay here!"

Angus had known she would offer again even before he'd opened his mouth. Half of him was happy to spend more time with her, but – and it was a big but – he was still uneasy about taking anything from her. On the other hand, he didn't mind staying in the poshest house in Topsham. *But should I? Is it wise?*

His hesitation made her stand up and come over. "I've got a fabulous guest room. It has an en-suite with the most amazing steam power shower and a Volcanic Limestone bath. Do you want to see it?"

She walked out of the room and Angus found himself following. He didn't need convincing, though: he'd already decided to accept. Three months ago, she'd gone away on holiday after a gruelling case: the one where her leg had been broken. While she'd visited some exotic island, Angus had had a chance to examine his growing feelings.

Seeing her come back tanned and glowing confirmed what he had already realised: things were about to get complicated in their relationship. His feelings had changed – they'd grown stronger.

Charlotte led him upstairs and opened the door to one of the rooms. It was exquisitely decorated. Someone, possibly Charlotte herself, had lavished attention to detail on every aspect. There was a huge bed with cream and white linen and extra cushions of the same colour. The headboard was cream and scalloped, the walls a darker cream, with the central section a grey and white flower pattern. The centrepiece was an ornate chandelier. Angus pointed at it. "Is that real?"

Charlotte looked up. "Of course it's real."

"No, I mean real crystal."

"Oh, I see what you mean. Yes, it is. I got Francois de la Rivière to design the bedrooms for me.

Angus shook his head with a smile. "I have no idea who that is."

She looked at him and blinked twice. "Never mind, it doesn't matter. Here, have a look at the bathroom. It's gorgeous." She pointed at another door, and he opened it.

To say that the bathroom was plush was an understatement. It was terracotta-coloured, and at the rear was a large shower cubicle with a Roman-style mosaic.

"I got the mosaic done especially," said Charlotte. "It's a copy of a real mosaic I saw in the Roman museum in St Albans."

Angus looked back at her. "It's lovely."

"You really like it?"

He smiled. "What's not to like?"

"You're welcome to stay as long as you want."

He moved further into the bathroom and saw a large white bath with ornate taps. His home would feel like a complete let-down when he went back to it.

"Thank you. All right, I'll collect what I need for a few days and stay while they dispose of the bomb."

Charlotte clapped her hands. "Excellent! Mi casa, su casa. We're going to be roommates!"

He raised his eyebrows, "Roommates? Are you moving in here, too?"

She nudged him with her elbow. "You know what I mean."

Angus wasn't sure how he felt. Charlotte had a habit of turning up at his house at unexpected times, and he often encountered her in unexpected places. Would that happen when they were in the same house? He imagined various embarrassing situations, mainly involving him being surprised in his underwear, or less.

"Charlotte," he said firmly, "there is one thing that I need you to do while I'm staying here."

"What's that?"

"Knock before you enter."

She smiled. "Of course."

Chapter Three

Angus left Charlotte's shortly afterwards to collect his belongings. The police let him through the cordon and he parked on his driveway.

The street was eerily quiet and he took a moment to look around at the other houses and there was no sign of anyone else.

He went inside and headed for the bedroom to pack clothes. He'd take enough for a week, that should be enough: jeans, two suits, seven shirts, some T-shirts, his running gear, trainers and his pyjamas and underwear.

Then he took the perishable items from the fridge, packed them in a bag and set off back to Charlotte's.

When he arrived, Charlotte let him in.

"I'd better get you a key and let you know the code for the burglar alarm. It's 01000011: binary for the capital letter C."

Angus stared at her. He wasn't sure he'd be able to remember that. Before he could say anything, Charlotte continued. "I've traced the IP address of the blackmailer. It was hard: most of the messages were behind a VPN, so it was almost impossible to trace, but I knew they'd slip up somewhere and they did."

Angus put his case at the foot of the stairs and followed her to the study.

"I worked out who was providing the VPN to the server. It was a cheap, shoddy company set up by complete amateurs."

Angus stood, watching her. He recognised the glint in her eye. It appeared whenever she'd cracked a tough computing case. He'd also started to realise that most people were amateurs, compared to Charlotte. He knew about VPNs: Virtual Private Networks. They encrypted your internet connection, therefore hiding everything you did online. "And?"

"Well, I hacked their server and discovered they'd—"

Angus put his hand up. "Woah. You hacked their server?"

Charlotte shrugged. "Well, it's based in Russia, so it's not like the UK government will care about it..." She had a point. "Anyway, they keep all the data on everyone using their software – probably to try and use it to their own advantage in the future. It's unethical and any legitimate VPN provider wouldn't do something like this. I downloaded the data without them knowing, trawled through it, and found the IP address of the evil messenger."

"The evil messenger?" Angus laughed.

Charlotte raised her eyebrows. He wasn't sure if she was going to laugh or slap him. "Blackmailing and sending threatening messages is pretty evil, in my opinion."

Angus paused. That was true, but it was still amusing. Charlotte had a way of coming up with the funniest phrases and he couldn't help but smile. "So, what did the IP address of the messenger tell you?"

"They've been sending messages from an address in Exeter."

"OK, but I thought IP addresses could change?"

"Says the technophobe! Yes, very good, they can. But if it's from a private address or business, they rarely do. I'd guess this is the same person, especially as it was just a couple of weeks ago."

"What's the address?"

"It's in St Thomas, and if you have a look at Google Maps, it's in the middle of a row of Victorian terraces."

"You've already looked?"

"Of course."

"And I assume you've searched for who lives there already?"

Charlotte nodded. Angus wondered if there was anything left for him to do: Charlotte seemed to have done it all.

"His name is David Saunders," she said. "I've done a quick search on him and found some basic info. He owns a few properties in the area and he's the director of a number of businesses in the city. I made a dossier." She handed him a number of printed A4 pages. "He's not big on social media. He has a Facebook profile, but he hasn't posted for a couple of years."

Angus glanced at the wad of paper. "All that while I was out collecting my clothes. Right, that's well outside the bomb cordon. We'll watch the house and get photos to make sure it actually is that person. Then we can show the rugby club. I'll get my camera." Angus started towards his suitcase.

"I'll bring my computer and have a sniff around their network," Charlotte replied.

Angus turned. "If you do that, we won't be able to give whatever you find to the rugby club."

"I know," she said with an innocent face. "But we can see what else he's up to."

An hour later, they were sitting in Angus's VW Golf, a few yards from the address but with full view of the the street. The row of Victorian houses was typical of many in the central part of the city and this house was in the middle of the row.

"That's very rebellious of you." Charlotte pointed to the sign a few yards away that said *Permit Parking Only*.

Angus turned off the engine. "I have been known to bend the rules when it helps with a case."

Charlotte took out her tablet and set to work to first isolate the network, then break into it.

Angus glanced at the computer screen. "There must be over thirty different home Wi-Fi accounts in that list."

"But I know the IP address, so it won't take long to find it." A few minutes later, she said, "Yep, got it."

Charlotte typed something and sat back. "Now I just have to wait, and see if my program can get into his network."

She put the computer on her lap. It was about a minute later when she spoke. "How long do you think it will be before he comes out of the house?"

Angus kept his gaze fixed on the front door. "I have no idea. He might not even be in. He could be at work."

Charlotte checked her watch. "It's 4.15. It could be hours before he's home."

"Yes."

A long silence fell. Eventually, Charlotte broke it. "Don't you get bored, just sitting here like this?"

"Sometimes." Angus glanced across at her. "I quite like just sitting doing nothing: it's almost like meditation. If you're with someone else – if they're annoying, for example – it either makes it bearable, or not."

Charlotte didn't reply at first. Then, as his words sank in, she turned towards him and stared. "What are you trying to tell me? Am I annoying?"

"I didn't mean you!"

She narrowed her eyes. "Are you sure? Because I'd rather you were honest. I don't want some hidden feelings to fester. Do you secretly hate me?"

"Don't be silly. If I found you annoying to sit with in situations like this, Charlotte, you wouldn't be here. I'd have come alone."

She faced the windscreen and took a deep breath. "All right. I know you well enough by now to know when you're speaking the truth. You can't lie."

Angus hoped she wouldn't take the matter further, such as asking how he felt about her beyond stakeout situations. He had, it was true, found her annoying to start with, especially when they first began working together. But lately his annoyance wasn't at her behaviour: it was that the things he used to find annoying were now endearing.

He stared out of the window, then picked up his phone and opened the news app. Distracting himself was the best option. Scrolling through it, he saw an article in the national news about the bomb in Exeter. *World War 2 bomb found in Exeter garden: thousands evacuated.*

The article was concise: just the facts about the bomb, not much more than he already knew.

"It's strange that bombs are still being found so long after the war ended," said Charlotte. "I wonder how many more there are in the UK?" Angus realised he didn't even mind that she'd looked at his phone screen.

"It's worse in Germany. One person every year is killed there by an unexploded World War 2 bomb."

"Really? That's terrible!" Charlotte tapped at her computer screen. "Hmm. He clearly has a strong password on his Wi-Fi: I haven't cracked it yet. I usually get them in less than two minutes."

"We might have to take the old-fashioned approach and just watch him."

She gave him a sidelong glance. "I hope not, but it would be easier to just knock on the door to try and find out if the registered owner lives there."

"Let's see if you can find out first. It's better we don't have direct contact. If we need to follow him in future, identifying ourselves isn't the best approach.

Over an hour later, Charlotte still hadn't hacked the Wi-Fi and there had been no sign of anyone entering or leaving the house.

Angus rubbed his eyes. "I'm going to get a coffee from that cafe down the road. Want one?"

"Yes. Decaf, please." She smiled.

"Phone me straight away if there's any movement." He got out the car, and she watched him walk down the road.

Charlotte stared at the screen on her tablet computer. The display showed the number of password combinations it had tried already. It was increasing quickly, but the brute-force attack hadn't found the correct one yet. It didn't usually take this long.

Charlotte's search tool included a dictionary search and a list of leaked passwords she had obtained from the dark web. Yes, it was illegal, but it had proved invaluable on many occasions and she only used it during investigations. She'd never use it to do anything bad herself.

Charlotte eyed the front door. She was sure she could get his name if he answered it. It would be better if she could hack it, but that might take days.

She considered pretending to be from the electric company; that had worked a while ago. But then she had another idea. She put her computer under the car seat and got out. If she was quick, she could get his name before Angus returned. Then they could go home and she could search him on the internet. She knocked on the door and waited. Nothing.

She knocked again, this time louder. There was a doorbell, so she pushed that too.

"What are you doing?"

Charlotte jumped and her heart pounded. She turned, slowly.

It was Angus.

"I thought you were getting coffee," she murmured.

"The cafe was closed."

"I'm going to ask him who he is."

"I leave the car for five minutes and you do this!"

"It's quicker this way," her voice was still low.

Angus opened his mouth, but before he could say anything, they heard footsteps. Then the door opened.

"Can I help?" The man in the doorway was in his early forties, wearing faded black jeans and a pale-blue shirt. His brown hair was unkempt and he had a few days' stubble.

"Hello," Charlotte said brightly. "My name is Sandra Butterworth and this is Greg Smith. We're from the council and we need to speak to Mr David Saunders. Is that you?"

"No, that's not me. That's the man who owns this house." He glanced at Angus, then back at Charlotte.

"Oh, that's a shame." She took out her phone and pretended to swipe the screen. "Do you know where he is? It's just that my list here says he owns a house in the area that has been sectioned off because of the World War 2 bomb they've found there. We need to check a few things with him. Are you sure he's not here?" Charlotte tried to look past him into the house but he was in the way.

The man looked interested. "Yeah, I heard about that. He has a house there? He never said."

"Could you give me his phone number? Then we can talk to him."

"All right, I'll just get it." He disappeared into the house, leaving the door open a crack.

Charlotte pushed the door gently, but when it opened, all she could see was the hall. She turned to Angus, who had remained silent. But from his expression, he wasn't happy.

The man returned holding a small piece of paper with a number written on it and handed it to Charlotte.

"Thank you so much, Mr...."

"James."

Charlotte held up her phone. "Could you tell me your full name, please? I need it for my boss. He's a stickler for logging information, especially if we can't contact Mr Saunders before they deal with the bomb."

James paused, as if assessing whether he should give his name. "Finley. James Finley. I'm his tenant."

"James Finley." Charlotte glanced at Angus, hoping he'd write the name down in the notebook he carried everywhere, but he made no movement. She typed it into the notes app on her phone. "Well, thank you, Mr Finley. Have a nice rest of your day." She beamed at him. He gave her a nod, then shut the door.

Charlotte stood for a moment, looking at the door knocker, and then turned to Angus.

He began to walk to the car. Charlotte hurried to catch up with him.

"Greg Smith?" Angus said, once they were inside the car.

"It was the first name I could think of." She shrugged. "It's a bit boring, I suppose. But we got his name and now we can look into him."

Angus gripped the steering wheel and stared out at the street ahead.

Charlotte swivelled to face him. "You're mad at me, aren't you? For knocking on the door. I knew you would be."

Angus was silent for a while, then took a deep breath. "I've told you before that we don't make direct contact with a surveillance target unless we absolutely have to."

"We did have to: we needed to find out who he was."

"You know what I mean." He turned to her. "I hate it when you go rogue on me. I'm the one who's leading the investigation, not you."

"But I got the results we needed and saved us a huge amount of time. I don't see the problem. Or is this about your ego? Are you annoyed that I got his name and you didn't?"

He stared at her. "Really? You're going there? You think I have a massive ego that needs massaging?"

"No, but I'm starting to wonder why you're so mad at me over this. If it isn't ego, what is it?"

"I'm annoyed because you didn't listen. If we need to follow him or do further surveillance, he'll recognise us now." He started the car.

"We can wear disguises." Charlotte countered.

Angus pressed the accelerator and drove off.

Chapter Four

They drove back in complete silence. Once in the house, Angus went straight to his room. It was getting late, and he was hungry. Possibly hangry, in fact, because he was so annoyed at Charlotte.

He lay down on the bed and looked up at the chandelier above him.

It felt strange being in one of Charlotte's bedrooms, like staying in an expensive hotel. He thought about staying at a friend's house instead, then remembered the en-suite bathroom and decided to give it a day or two. It shouldn't take that long for the bomb to be dealt with. He got up, put his suitcase on the bed and started to unpack.

He was halfway through when his phone rang. The display said it was Rhona, his ex-wife. That was all he needed.

Angus contemplated not answering. It had been a while since he'd spoken to her.

He decided to answer. "Rhona. Long time no speak." He carried on taking things out of his suitcase with his free hand.

"Angus, how are you? I just saw the map of the evacuation zone for the bomb and your house is in it. I wanted to check you were ok."

Angus took a small pile of shirts over to the wardrobe. "Yes, I'm packed and out of the area already."

"Have you got somewhere to stay, or did they allocate you accommodation?"

"I'm staying with a friend."

"Graham?" He could hear voices in the background: she was still at work.

"No."

"Oh, I know – you're staying with that multi-millionaire girlfriend of yours. The blonde. Which of her fifteen houses are you in?"

"That's not a very nice thing to say, Rhona. Charlotte only has one house, though it's a very nice one. And as a matter of fact, I am staying with her. Not that it's any of your business."

Rhona said nothing for a few seconds. "As your councillor, I'm just making sure you've got a roof over your head."

"It's very kind of you Rhona. Thank you."

Angus sat on the edge of the bed and stared at the carpet in front of him. "You're not actually my councillor, Rhona. I'm not in your ward. But it's kind of you to ring and check on me."

"Just because we're divorced, it doesn't mean I don't care about you."

"I'd better let you go. I'm sure you have a hundred things to organise and worry about, and I don't need to be one of them."

"Alright. Bye, then." She said abruptly.

Angus ended the call and put his phone on the bed. A TV was attached to the wall opposite, and he switched it on for company. He changed channel until he found something of interest: Viper's Nest. An episode without Charlotte's ex-husband Idris.

"Knock knock," said Charlotte's voice from the crack in the door. "Can I come in?"

He picked up the remote control and switched off the TV, "Yes."

"Are you still mad at me?"

He sighed and sat on the bed. She did the same.

"Not any more, but don't do that again."

"All right. Have you got everything you need?"

He nodded. "I think so."

"Well, let me know if there is anything. This room overlooks the back garden, so you won't get any noise from the road. Or the river."

"I'm sure it will be quiet enough."

She paused, thinking. "Would you like a room overlooking the river?" She indicated the other side of the house. "There are a couple of rooms on that side but none of them have an en suite. Maybe I should convert one and make it into a bathroom for the other..."

"This room is perfect, thanks. I don't need a view of the river."

"If you change your mind, you can just swap. The bathroom is at the end of the corridor. It's similar to this one, except that it's in the Greek style."

"How many bathrooms do you have?"

"Four. The en suite in this room, one in my room, and the one next to this, although that's more of a shower room. Plus the main bathroom and the downstairs toilet."

"That must be a cleaning nightmare."

Charlotte blinked at him.

"Not for you. I mean for whoever cleans them."

Charlotte shrugged. "My cleaner gets paid a lot more than the standard rate. Anyway, most of them don't get used very often."

He stood up, zipped up the empty suitcase and put it against the wall. "Well, I don't know about you, but I'm ready for dinner. How about I cook us something? Have you got much in?"

Charlotte blinked at him again. "I have no idea. Helena deals with all that, but she should have some ingredients in."

"I'll take a look."

In the kitchen, Angus looked in all the cupboards. There was a good range of food: tins and packets, pasta and rice, herbs and spices. In the fridge, there was salad, a few vegetables, smoothies and lots of milk. No meat or fish. He took out an onion, peppers and carrots, and set to work.

Charlotte came into the kitchen ten minutes later as Angus was stirring a frying pan full of gently simmering passata and vegetables. "That smells lovely." She was carrying a bottle of beer and handed it to him.

"Thanks." He took a sip and put it on the counter. "Have you started looking into James Finley yet?"

Charlotte shook her head. "As tempting as it was, I'm trying to achieve a healthy work-life balance. I decided to leave it until tomorrow morning."

A pan of hot water came to the boil. Angus adjusted the temperature, then picked up a packet of pasta and poured some into the water. "Fair enough. It's not like this is time-sensitive."

"What did you think of him when you saw him?"

"Well, he was neat but scruffy."

"How so?"

"He had several days' stubble and he hadn't combed his hair. However, his shirt cuffs were buttoned rather than rolled up."

"Which isn't scruffy."

"No, but he hadn't tucked his shirt in."

"Shocking." Charlotte grinned. "But very observant. I didn't notice that."

"It could indicate that he does video conferences or Zoom meetings and has to look smart."

"But his hair was messy."

Angus stirred the pasta. "True. Well, we'll find out tomorrow."

Ten minutes later, they were sitting at the dining table eating vegetable pasta.

"If you cook like this for me every night, you can stay for good." Charlotte smiled.

Angus stopped chewing for a moment and glanced at her. The thought of staying here every night was suddenly more appealing. They'd been working together for a long time now and eaten together countless times. This felt different and he couldn't put his finger on why.

"Have you ever considered learning to cook?" he asked.

"God, no!" Charlotte said immediately. "I know how to cook – a few things, anyway. But I hate it and I'm bad at it."

"It's all down to practice."

"I'm just not willing to put the effort in. Anyway, who were you talking to on the phone earlier? You had the grumpiest expression."

"Rhona."

"Ah, my least favourite councillor. What did she want?"

"She was checking I'd found somewhere to stay, because she'd realised I lived near the bomb site."

"How sweet. Did she offer you a bed with her and whoever she's seeing?"

"No, she was just glad I'd found somewhere."

"Ooh, did you tell her you were staying with me?" Charlotte's eyes lit up. "Please tell me you did! I bet she called me your 'blonde bit' again." Charlotte was smiling like a Cheshire Cat.

Angus sat back in his chair and took a swig of beer. "I did tell her, yes, and I'm not going to tell you what she said."

"Spoilsport."

"What does it matter?"

"She clearly still has feelings for you."

"It's purely platonic. We go way back. We don't hate each other."

Charlotte put down her fork and stared at him. "Why did you get divorced, then?"

He shrugged. "You know why. We just grew apart."

"She hasn't grown apart as much as you have." Charlotte said, then put a forkful of pasta into her mouth.

"We aren't getting back together, Charlotte. That part of our lives is over. We rarely have contact, but if we do, it's always civil."

Charlotte looked at Angus. "OK," she said, eventually.

She liked the thought of having Angus in the house permanently. It was reassuring. That made her inner feminist cringe for a moment. She didn't need a man to look after her – or did she? Maybe it was just that she missed the companionship of a relationship. Maybe she should get herself out there... She glanced at Angus, who smiled at her as best he could while eating. Somehow, the thought of a different man sitting next to her just didn't feel right.

She needed to stop acting like a love-sick teenager and focus on enjoying having Angus in the house 24/7. If something was ever going to happen between them, it would happen. She had to trust that it would.

The next morning, Charlotte was making a coffee when Angus came in. He was smartly dressed in his usual suit trousers and a shirt, but no tie. He had shaved, and as he passed her, she caught a whiff of his cologne, Sauvage by Christian Dior. She'd tracked it down months ago visiting John Lewis in Exeter and smelling all of the men's colognes one by one until she'd found it. It had taken nearly an hour from start to finish and when she'd identified it, she'd bought bottle of the most expensive potency as a reward. Then she realised she couldn't give it to him and it would be slightly creepy keeping it, so she'd donated it to the charity shop in town.

"Coffee?" she asked, taking a sip from her own mug.

"I'll make it." He went to the machine and pressed the Americano button.

"Did you sleep well? Was the bed comfortable?"

"It was, and I slept like a baby." There was a pause in the conversation as the coffee machine made its usual noises. Angus poured milk into the cup when it had finished. "So, will we start looking into James Finley this morning?"

Charlotte shook her head, her blonde hair rippling. "No need. I couldn't get to sleep last night, so I started to investigate James. It was a bit tricky at first, but I've found out a lot."

Angus, who had been about to sip his coffee, froze, then put the mug down. "So it's all done?"

"Yep. For now." She handed him a few printed pages stapled in the top left-hand corner. "It's all in there, although I'm guessing there's more to find out. By three am I was ready to sleep."

Angus glanced at the first sheet, trying to suppress the feeling that he was a spare wheel in the partnership. He pushed it aside and started to read.

Name: James Philip Finley, aged 41, born Tilbury, Wiltshire. No known criminal convictions.

Marital status: single

Siblings: one older brother, Michael, who emigrated to Australia four years ago. He works as an engineer for a company called Marine Assets.

Education: Tilbury High School (11 GCSEs), Wiltshire College of Further Education (three A Levels in Accountancy, Maths and Further Maths).

Current work: Business planning and strategic funding consultant for KOP International.

There followed a list of his social-media accounts, with their handles, and a sample of his typical posts.

"Nothing out of the ordinary here," Angus commented.

Charlotte nodded. "It's all very tame, isn't it? But this is just a front. If you turn the page, I've added some posts from his other accounts – the trolling accounts – to the club."

Angus turned the page and his eyes widened. The contrast was striking. Anime avatars, swearing, and abusive, hateful comments. "He's got quite the split personality, hasn't he?"

"Yep."

"Are you sure this is the same person?"

Charlotte, who was just sipping her coffee, spluttered and nearly spat it out. She put her cup down and stared at Angus. "I shall pretend you didn't say that."

"It's not that I don't trust you, Charlotte, but we need hard evidence that this is him."

"I have hard evidence: it's in the document. The IP addresses are the same. Or rather, they're different, but they all come from the same place – his house."

"Because you hacked the VPN."

"Yes. Every time he uses it, it needs to know where he is. All the messages come from his home, so it must be him."

"Unless someone else lives there too. We need to check whether that's the case and watch his house."

"I'll try and hack his Wi-Fi again. We can leave whenever you like – although would you like breakfast first? I suppose there's no need to rush if he works from home." Charlotte sighed. "I can't believe I didn't ask him whether anyone else lived there."

Angus sipped his coffee, musing. He should have asked that, too, but now it was too late. They'd have to live with the consequences and watch the house again.

However, if they were going to stake out the house, Angus wanted to do it alone. They'd probably be there all day, and sitting in the car with Charlotte would be tricky. Not only because he had a growing suspicion that she suffered from some form of undiagnosed ADHD, but also because he was getting far too comfortable with her invading every aspect of his life.

Yet instead of telling her to stay at home because he'd deal with it, he found himself saying "I'll just have some toast and we can leave in about fifteen minutes. Probably better to take your Volvo, in case he saw my car yesterday."

Chapter Five

An hour later, they sat watching the same house as they had the day before. Charlotte was more subdued than she had been earlier, concentrating on the tablet computer as she tried to hack James Finley's Wi-Fi. "I'll try a different algorithm today: one I tweaked last night. Have you heard any more about the bomb?" She was tapping the screen as she spoke.

"They've just told me to sit tight. But I've checked the fine print of my house insurance and surprise surprise, it doesn't include bombs."

That made Charlotte look up at him. "I'm guessing that's not something you can add now."

Angus snorted. "No insurance company will cover that."

"Why don't you give your ex a call about it? You'd think the council would have that side of things covered."

Angus pondered her words for a moment. "I'll text her."

His thumbs were poised over his phone when a man in his mid twenties, wearing tight-fitting jeans and a bomber jacket, walked past them and stopped outside James's house. He had short brown hair, neatly styled, although the top looked as if it tended to curls.

Charlotte and Angus looked at each other. "Isn't he one of the rugby players from the club?" Charlotte asked.

"Yes." Angus sat up, took the camera from his lap, and snapped some photos. The door opened and the man disappeared inside.

Charlotte was already on the rugby club website, looking through the list of players. "Oliver Miller?" She held the photo up to Angus.

"Yes, that's him," said Angus.

"Transferred from Cheltenham two years ago," Charlotte read from the screen. "Twenty-seven years old. I wonder why he's visiting the house of a man who is threatening the club?"

Angus took out his notebook and wrote down Oliver's name. "It's deeply suspicious. Also, we can't rule out that he might be sending the messages. I'll need you to check for any new messages and the time they were sent."

Charlotte shrugged a shoulder. "Emails and messages can be scheduled. We'd need more proof."

"True, but they might not be scheduling them."

"What do you think they're doing?"

"I don't like to speculate. We can't assume it's bad. It could be that they're friends and don't know what each other get up to in their own time."

"If I can just get into James's Wi-Fi, I'll be able to get to the bottom of it."

They sat quietly, watching the door, until another man approached from the other side of the road and stopped outside the house. He was dressed in light-grey sweatpants and a dark-grey hoody, pulled up.

"What is it about hoodies that makes anyone look suspicious?" Charlotte commented.

He rang the doorbell, and a few moments later, stepped inside.

As soon as Angus had seen the man coming, he'd picked up his camera. When the man had disappeared inside, he showed Charlotte a close-up on the small display.

"I'll check the club website again." Charlotte scrolled through the team photos. "He's not here: I'll try the coaches." She scrolled further down. "Wow, they have more coaches than players. A scrum coach, a kicking coach, a line-out coach. Can you imagine the careers advice at school? 'What do you want to do for a job, little Jonny?' 'I want to be a kicking coach.'"

She scrolled again. "Ah, here he is. Lee Clarke, Forwards Coach."

Angus wrote that in his notebook. "Quite the little gathering, so far."

A movement in the wing mirror caught Charlotte's eye: another man was walking towards them. "Incoming behind us," she told Angus. He didn't move, but waited for the person to pass. This man was dressed in jeans and a smart long-sleeved shirt. Once he had gone by, Angus lifted his camera to take photos. Sure enough, the man stopped at James's, knocked, and went in.

Charlotte searched the club website, but couldn't find him. "If he works at the club, he could be a different type of member of staff. Admin, or something like that."

"I'll ask Trevor. Interesting that no one's brought anything with them." Angus commented.

"What do you mean?"

"That makes it unlikely to be a social gathering. None of them have brought food or drink."

"Good point."

Angus kept watching and didn't say anything else.

They sat in silence for another ten minutes. Charlotte watched her computer screen and Angus staring at the house. A red family-sized car drove down and stopped in the middle of the street. A man got out, went straight to James's house and knocked on the door. Moments later, he disappeared inside.

Charlotte looked over at Angus. "Did you get a photo of him?"

Angus looked at the small screen on the back of the camera. "Just about."

They looked at the shots. The man's profile was blurred, but Charlotte went back to the rugby website and searched through the players again. "I think that's Tom Hunter," she pointed to a head shot of the player.

"You're right."

Angus wrote the names in his notebook. "Two players, one coach, and an unknown man, all descending on James. How many more do you think will turn up?"

"I wonder why they didn't meet at the club?"

"Either this isn't related to the club or they don't want anyone else to know that they're meeting. I'd guess the latter."

Charlotte looked at her tablet. "I still can't get into the Wi-Fi. If I could, I'd at least know what they're up to. He's bound to have something I can hack, and I'd be able to look at his private messages."

It was an hour before there was any further movement at James's house. No one else had arrived or left, but eventually the front door opened and all the men apart from James spilled onto the pavement. They walked in the same direction until three went right and one left.

Angus turned to Charlotte. "I'll follow the three: you take the car and follow the one who went left. I'll call you." He started to get out of the car, hesitated and turned back to her. "Remember, just follow him. Don't engage with him in any way. Promise?"

"Promise.".

Angus disappeared up the street.

Chapter Six

Charlotte watched Angus stride down the road. Then she remembered she needed to follow the other man. She started the car, pulled out and turned left. She could just see the man in the distance. It was Oliver Miller, the first man they'd seen enter James's house. He walked quickly, but it wouldn't take her long to catch up and pass him.

She thought about slowing down, but a small white van appeared in her rear-view mirror. Cursing it, she drove past Oliver. As soon as she could, she pulled over and let the white van pass. It revved its engine at her as it went by. "Oh, I'm so sorry for driving at a decent speed in a built-up area," she said, in a sarcastic tone.

The name of the company was on the back of the van: *Devon Grows Fruit and Veg.* "I'll never buy anything from you."

She drummed her fingers on the steering wheel and checked her rear-view mirror for Oliver. She could see him in the distance, so switched off the engine and waited until he'd passed, pretending to be on the phone. Once he was almost out of sight, she followed him again, driving slowly and hoping that nobody would drive up behind her.

He turned right, going away from the city centre. She tried not to pass him, but another car came up behind her. She pulled over and let it pass, then waited until she thought she could stay behind him.

She thought following him on foot, but he was walking quickly and her previously broken leg still hurt if she walked too much.

She was saved from further debate as he turned right again, then slowed down and stopped outside a detached bungalow. As Charlotte drove past, she saw him pull out a key and let himself in. "Must be your home," she thought. As soon as she could, she pulled over and made a note of the address.

When Angus got out of the car, he strode off quickly. He could hear the three men talking, but he was too far away to make out what they were saying.

They were walking north, towards the city centre. Angus followed at a safe distance. After half a mile, they stopped. The unknown man walked one way, the coach and Tom Hunter another. Who should he follow? With moments to decide, he went for the unknown man.

He had left his camera in the car with Charlotte, but it would be far too obvious to take photos now. He felt in his pocket for his mobile phone, just in case. The unknown man put his hand in his pocket too and took out a packet of cigarettes. He paused for a moment, then moved on, a puff of smoke trailing behind him.

Fifteen minutes later, they were almost in the centre of the city. The man turned right by St Sidwell's church. Angus slowed down and watched him enter the graveyard. But instead of pausing at one of the gravestones, he kept walking, disappearing through a hole in the wire fence at the back. Angus blinked, then followed. He came out at the rear of a small, two-storey industrial building. On its side, in fading letters, was the company name: *Comm Fab*. Angus didn't recognise the name, and he didn't think he'd ever been on this street before. The man walked round to the main entrance and went in.

Angus walked past the building and stopped further up the road, making sure he could still see the entrance. He searched for Comm Fab on his phone and found its website, which stated that it was a community interest company that '*Helps the community in many ways*.' That could mean anything.

There were a lot of photos showing different groups of smiling people, with their names underneath. But there were no photos which included the man he'd been tailing.

No one was about, so Angus decided to wait where he was and pretend to be on the phone if anyone did walk by. He didn't have to wait long: a few minutes later, the unknown man left the building with another man of similar age and appearance. They walked round the building to a small car park, got into a blue Ford and drove off. Angus memorised the number plate, then wrote it in his notebook once the car had gone. He had been tempted to take a photo of the pair, but that would have been like standing with a big sign saying "*Look at me*".

Charlotte was just about to message Angus when a text arrived.

Followed the unknown man but he's gone off in car with a friend. Are you done?

Charlotte replied: *Yes, followed Oliver to his home. Where are you? I'll pick you up.*

He sent her a What3Words location, and she smiled. It hadn't been so long since she had used it to get out of a very tricky situation.

A few minutes later, she pulled up at his location and he got into the car.

"Shall we go home?" she asked.

"Yes. There's no use in hanging around, and we need to discuss what we've discovered."

It took about twenty minutes to get back to Topsham. During the drive, Charlotte realised that Angus hadn't complained at her use of the word *home*. Technically, she supposed her home was also his at the moment, too. She liked that; it gave her a warm feeling. She wasn't quite sure how she would let him go.

Back at the house, Angus told her what he had seen when following the unknown man. "He's not on the Comm Fab website. He was in the building for a few minutes, presumably met someone there, and then went off with them."

"I've never heard of Comm Fab. What sort of community things does it do?"

"I hadn't heard of it either. It looks pretty run down. I'd guess they don't get much money."

"Community projects like that never get much." As part of her philanthropic endeavours, Charlotte had given a lot of money to the smaller, less glamorous charities and groups.

"I'll have a look on Companies House and see what I can find." Angus took his camera from the camera bag, ejected the SD card and handed it to Charlotte. "Can you see if the photos I took of him are any help in working out who he is?"

Charlotte nodded. A few minutes later, she'd printed photos of everyone who had been at the meeting, with their names, and pinned it on her conspiracy board.

Angus had been watching Charlotte at intervals as he did research on the Companies House website. When she had finished pinning all the photos and names he went over to it. "Now all we need to do is figure out why they were meeting."

"Yes, and why they were meeting at James's house in particular. I mean, if he's blackmailing the rugby club, do they know?"

"They might. Can you check whether there were any trolling messages while they were meeting?"

"Well, we already know the time doesn't matter. As I said, they can schedule the messages."

"Can you schedule private messages, though?"

"Not easily. But most of them were emails and those are very easy to schedule."

"All right" said Angus. "We'll assume that any messages sent then were scheduled."

He sat back down, and admitted to himself that it would have been much easier if Charlotte could have hacked into James's Wi-Fi and had a snoop around. He was starting to see how much easier hacking would make everything. It wasn't ethically sound, but it would help to solve the mystery much faster.

He was surprised at how he felt about hacking now. When he had first come across Charlotte and discovered that she hacked people's Wi-Fi networks, he'd been shocked and a little bit disgusted. Now, though, he'd learned it could be incredibly helpful. "I should try and recalibrate my ethics," he thought. In fact, if he was able to hack like Charlotte, he probably would, too. Anyway, she hadn't been able to hack James, so they would have to find out what was going on some other way.

He looked over to the board. "Our first priority is to find out the identity of the mystery man. I'll get a contact to search the number plate of the car they left in and see where that leads us."

"Is the contact my brother?" Charlotte asked. Mark "Woody" Lockwood was still a DCI in the Devon and Cornwall Police, despite Charlotte giving him a sizeable chunk of money when she became a multi-millionaire.

"No. Someone else who owes me a few favours."

Charlotte nodded. "Could your contact do a facial-recognition search?"

Angus shook his head. "I doubt it. That takes clearance, and I'm not sure that even Woody can do that. Plus if an officer is caught doing unauthorised facial searches for members of the public, it's a disciplinary offence. It's also rarer, and therefore much more obvious. A car number plate search can be explained away easily: those happen all the time."

Charlotte tapped her finger on the desk. "I wonder if there's a way for me to get into the facial-recognition software on the police servers."

Angus shook his head. "Don't even think about it."

Charlotte rolled her eyes. "I know, I know. I was just kidding. Hacking government websites and especially the police servers is a step too far, even for me. I'd end up in prison for a very long time. Worse still, I'd be banned from using the internet once I got out."

"Hmmm. Well, let's see what the number-plate check comes back with."

Angus picked up his phone and left the room. Charlotte started carrying out internet searches for each of the players, to get some background on them.

A few minutes later, Angus came back in. "The number plate's fake. It's from a vehicle scrapped about a year ago."

Charlotte looked up from her computer. "Well, that's definitely suspicious."

Angus sighed. "Yes, and it's a dead end."

"We need to go to this Comm Fab place and find someone who can identify him," said Charlotte. "Shall we go together?"

Angus nodded. "We'll go in my car."

A few minutes later, they were heading back into Exeter. Charlotte took out her tablet and started tapping at the screen.

Angus glanced over. "What are you doing?"

"Getting some info on the people who run Comm Fab. If we've got names, and maybe a bit more, we can pretend to be something other than private investigators."

Angus frowned, then concentrated on the road ahead. "Why would you want to pretend that you aren't a private investigator?"

"Mr Unknown might be a nasty piece of work. He might even come after us. We now know that he meets up with people who are threatening the rugby club, and he has a friend with a stolen number plate on his car. Not a good start, is it?"

Angus had to agree. "So if we go in and start asking questions, what will you say? I mean, who will we say we are?"

"We can say we're from the council again: it seems to

work. The council have so many workers in so many departments that if Comm Fab do phone up and try to check us out, they'll probably get lost in the phone system."

Charlotte scrolled down her screen and showed Angus a photo of a middle-aged woman. "This is from the 'about us' page of the website. Meet Muriel Jones. She's a paragon of virtue: she worked as a nurse in the NHS and used to run an old people's home. She does lots for charity, and I quote, 'loves helping the community in any way I can.' I'm sure she'll accept a sizeable donation in exchange for information about Mr Unknown."

"In other words, you're going to throw your money around to get information." Angus realised as he spoke the words that his tone was harsher than he had intended. "If you give bribes out every time you want information, you'll run through your money pretty quickly."

"No I won't. What I have in mind would be a drop in the ocean: a small donation to the centre, which to them would mean a lot."

Angus tried to suppress his negative feelings about Charlotte's seemingly limitless resources but he found himself challenging her. "Instead of bribing Muriel Jones, why don't you try getting the information through asking and investigation? Look on it as a challenge: a new way of working."

Charlotte gave him a sidelong glance. "I'm not sure I like the sound of that." She could afford a donation and it would probably make things easier and quicker. They both knew it.

"Just give it a try."

"What about the centre, though? They could do with the money. They have a JustGiving page where they're always asking for donations."

"How about this, then?" said Angus. "If you get the info you need without bribing them, leave an anonymous donation on their page afterwards."

"What if you find out the information?"

"If either of us finds it. The whole point is not to fall back on a bribe."

"All right, challenge accepted," Charlotte replied. "I mean, I can get information without a bribe. It's just easier to flash money at people. Everyone has a price, you know." She smiled at Angus.

"What?" he asked.

"I'm just wondering what your price is," she said, and her smile broadened to a grin.

Chapter Seven

When they arrived at Comm Fab, Angus parked in the exact spot he'd seen the unknown man leave from earlier. As they got out of the car, Charlotte indicated that he should lead and she would follow.

The interior of the building was as shabby as the outside. The worn orange carpet looked from the mid-nineties and the walls were dirty with chipped white paint. The corridor in front of them showed a room to the left, a room to the right, and a kitchen area straight ahead. Inside the entrance was a noticeboard headed *All Welcome,* and underneath, lots of posters advertising events in the building. There was also a A4 sheet with an event timetable.

Angus took photos of the noticeboard with his phone. That hadn't occurred to Charlotte, but she thought it was a good idea. They could analyse the information later. She inspected the board, looking for photographs of the people who volunteered there, but there were none.

Angus went into the room on the left-hand side and Charlotte followed. It was large, with tables set out and six chairs around each. Numerous people were sitting at the tables. She did a quick headcount: thirteen.

At the far end of the room was a large hatch opening on the kitchen. Several women with green tabards were in there. On the hatch counter were tea-things and a plate of biscuits.

A middle-aged woman in a tabard approached them. "Hello, can I help you?"

"We wondered if you knew this man?" Angus unfolded a printed copy of one of his photos and showed the lady.

She peered at it and shook her head. Angus watched her closely to see if there was a flicker of recognition, but nothing in her reaction suggested she knew the man.

"I haven't seen him before, but I'm new here. Debbie knows everyone, though. Debbie!" She called to another woman wearing a tabard, who was pouring cups of tea at the hatch.

Debbie looked up at the sound of her name, then put the large metal teapot down and came over. The other woman went off and Angus repeated his question.

Debbie looked at the photo, gave a tight smile and shook her head. "Sorry love, never seen him before." She returned to the hatch, picked up two cups of tea and took them to one of the tables.

Charlotte gave Angus a look that said, as plainly as words, 'She knows him.'

She whispered, "I'll ask some of the old folk." She took the photo, went to a table with a spare chair and sat down.

The four elderly ladies sitting there, who had been chatting quietly, all looked at her.

"Hello, I'm Charlotte. I wonder if I could ask you all a question?"

"Hello, dear," said one of the women. "Of course you

can ask me a question. I might not choose to answer it though." She gave Charlotte a cheeky smile.

"Well, let's see," Charlotte showed her the photo. "Have you seen this man in here at all?"

The woman took the photo and looked at it. "I need my glasses, really. Joan, can I borrow yours?"

The woman next to her bent down to her handbag, took out her reading glasses and gave them to her friend. She glanced at the photo. "He looks familiar. Do you know him, Bea?"

Bea studied the photo with the aid of the reading glasses. "Isn't that the man who comes in sometimes to help with the deliveries? Why do you want to know? Ooh, are you the police? Are you investigating?"

Charlotte hesitated, unsure what to say. She wanted to pretend to be from the council, as she and Angus had agreed beforehand, but she felt bad lying to them. "We're private investigators," she said at last.

"Private investigators? I've never met one of those before, and I'm ninety-six!"

Charlotte grinned. "Well, there's a first time for everything, even at your young age."

Bea looked towards Angus. "Is he a private investigator too?"

Charlotte winced, Bea had said it a little bit too loud and with a conspiratorial tone. "Yes, he's my partner."

"Handsome chap. If I were a few decades younger..."

Charlotte tapped the photo. "So, does anyone know his name?"

Another lady at the table wrinkled her nose. "They call him Screwball. He comes in here sometimes, but mostly he hangs around like a bad smell. I'm sure he's up to no good." Her tone was contemptuous.

Joan's eyes widened. "You can't say that, Mary! He just comes in sometimes. No harm in that."

Mary's mouth turned down in a grimace. "Like everyone else, he thinks old people like us are blind and deaf. But I take notice, and I've seen how people react when he's in the building, swaggering about. Everyone's tense when he's here, and relaxed when he's gone. I'm not surprised someone's looking into him. I'm sure if you dig a bit, you'll discover all sorts."

Charlotte glanced towards Angus, who was talking to an elderly man at another table. "Do you know why he's called Screwball?"

"No idea. I'm guessing he came up with the nickname himself to try and scare people. You know the sort of thing. Crusher, or Mad Dog."

"Or Knuckles, or Mad Hatter," Joan added.

"I knew a man called Johnny Sausage." Bea said. All the ladies laughed.

"Do you know anything else about Screwball?" Charlotte asked.

"No," said Mary. "But he's not liked. By anyone."

Joan scoffed at Mary's words, but said nothing. Charlotte had the feeling they'd be having words with each other after she'd gone.

"Thank you: you've been really helpful. It would be really good if you didn't let anyone know we were asking about him."

Mary gave a curt nod, then looked straight in front of her as though Charlotte wasn't there. One of the others tapped the side of her nose with her finger. "Mum's the word."

Charlotte stood up and went over to Angus. The elderly gentleman was speaking loudly, "In my day we didn't have time to run amok. We had to work hard to earn a crust. After we'd done our national service, that is. I was one of the last. It stopped the year after, but I'm glad I did it. Gave me discipline. The army was like a family to me. You don't get camaraderie like that anywhere else."

Angus sat listening until he caught sight of Charlotte nearby. A few moments later, he said goodbye to the man, stood up and approached her.

Charlotte lowered her voice. "He's known as Screwball but no one knows his real name or what the nickname means. Apparently he comes into the centre a lot and he's not well liked. No direct evidence, but his presence makes people uneasy."

"That would tie in with Debbie's reaction," said Angus.

"We could question others, but that carries a risk. Sooner or later, someone may mention that we were here asking about him. I told the ladies over there not to mention us, but there's no guarantee the others won't."

"Let's try and think of another way to find out who he is."

"I could ask Helena or Grigore to volunteer here. They might be able to find out more."

"Or you could volunteer."

"So could you," Charlotte shot back.

They stared at each other, neither giving ground.

"Now that we've both come here and asked questions," Charlotte said, eventually, "it would be safer for someone else to find out what they can."

Angus took a deep breath. "All right. Speak to them both and see if one of them is willing."

"OK. Shall we go?"

Angus nodded.

Once home, Charlotte phoned Helena but she'd said

she was too busy with the women's refuge over the next few days to help. So she went out to Grigore, who was in the garden on the ride-on mower. He stopped the engine as soon as he saw her and climbed off.

"You're such a sweetie, doing the lawn," she said, as soon as he took the ear protectors off.

"I like it," he said in his strong Romanian accent.

"Not as much as flying, I bet. How are the lessons going?"

"Good. I prefer airplane to helicopter."

"Really? Well, at least you know what to concentrate on."

"You vant somezing?"

"Yes. How do you feel about doing some infiltration for me?"

"OK. Vat I do?"

"I'd like you to volunteer at a community centre and find out as much as you can about a man who visits it." Charlotte filled him in on the case and their need to find out about Screwball.

"I go tomorrow and hang around to find out more."

"Thank you, Grigore! You could pretend you've just moved here and you're trying to make friends."

"I pretend I don't speak English. People zink I don't understand."

"Clever."

Charlotte went inside to tell Angus the good news and found him by the conspiracy board. He'd added Screwball's name underneath his photo.

"Good news! Grigore has agreed to go to the Comm Fab tomorrow. What should we do now?"

"We need to do a deep-dive analysis of all the other men

at the house. Find out everything we can. Something might give us a clue to why they were meeting."

Charlotte walked to her computer. "I'll keep going with Oliver Miller."

"Which ones haven't you done yet?" asked Angus. "I'll help."

Charlotte raised an eyebrow. "All right. You do the coach, Lee Clarke."

It was hours later before they both decided it was time to pack up work for the night and have something to eat. "Shall I call for a takeaway?" Charlotte asked. "You can't cook every night."

Angus looked up from his computer. "I don't mind cooking every night. I do it most nights anyway."

"There's a new Thai restaurant just opened in the town. I'd love to try it."

Half an hour later, the doorbell rang. "I'll get it," said Angus. He stood up, stretched, and headed for the door to get their food delivery. But the man at the door was in his thirties, dressed in smart jeans and a dark-blue shirt, and he didn't have a takeaway bag with him. He was holding a bunch of flowers. Angus looked past him to the red Ferrari parked on the drive.

The man stared at Angus, confusion on his face. "Er, hi, is she in?"

Angus planted his feet more firmly on the threshold. "She is, yes. And you are?"

"Ross, I'm a friend," he said in a thick east London accent. "Mind if I come in?"

So this was Ross. Charlotte's 'friend with benefits'. Angus sized him up. He was shorter than he imagined, that was gratifying, but he was good-looking and didn't have a grey hair in sight. He wanted to stop him entering, but it wasn't his house.

Reluctantly, Angus stepped aside and Ross entered. He headed straight for Charlotte's study. Angus followed, not quite sure of the etiquette.

Charlotte stood up as the door opened. "Ross!" she exclaimed. Ross gathered her in his arms, lifted her off the floor, and launched into a full-on kiss.

Seething jealousy coursed through Angus as he watched them. *That man's like a wolf who hasn't eaten for weeks,* he thought. He wondered whether Charlotte was kissing Ross back, but he couldn't look, because watching Charlotte kiss another man was worse than... Worse than what? Food poisoning? Definitely. Being shot at? Yes, because this kiss seemed to be going on for ever. Angus looked away and tried not to make a face.

Luckily, his torment was broken by the doorbell ringing again. *This must be the food,* he thought, with great relief.

He retreated to the door and took the delivery bag from the man, giving him a tip. "Thanks. Nice motor," the delivery man said, nodding at the Ferrari, then went back to his dark-green Skoda estate.

Angus closed the door and went straight to the kitchen. He put the takeaway bag on the table, trying not to think about Ross and Charlotte in the next room. *How far will they have got by now?*

He opened the cupboard to get some plates and Charlotte came in, carrying the flowers that Ross had brought. She put them on the counter, then silently got a vase from a cupboard, filled it with water, and put the flowers in. Angus glanced at them: flawless pink roses with just enough greenery to form a contrast.

Ross appeared at the kitchen door and leant on the frame. Angus could see a blush coming to Charlotte's cheeks. "Angus, this is Ross. Ross, this is Angus," she said, her voice higher than usual.

Ross came into the kitchen and stuck out a hand. "Pleased to meet you, Angus. Charlotte's mentioned you often, so it's nice to put a face to the name. Sorry about a moment ago: I thought you were staff when you answered the door."

Angus raised his eyebrows, but said nothing. He shook Ross's hand for just long enough not to be rude.

"I ordered far too much food, so there's plenty for us all." Charlotte began taking the foil food containers out of the bag and putting them on the counter.

Angus felt an overwhelming rush of emotion. What was it? Jealously, yes. But more than that. More like ... inadequacy. Ross was the friend Charlotte sometimes slept with, no strings attached. Ross was at least fifteen years younger than he was, with a Ferrari on the drive and probably millions in the bank. Angus, on the other hand, was an ex-police detective with a failed marriage, a VW Golf and a semi-detached house in Exeter.

"I'll take mine to my room so that you two can catch up." Angus took a plate and started to put food on it.

Charlotte stared at him. "Stay and eat with us, Angus: you won't be getting in the way. Ross just popped in because he was in the area."

Angus glanced at her, then Ross. If he'd been in Ross's position, he'd want Charlotte all to himself.

Ross gave him a curt nod. "Yeah."

Chapter Eight

Charlotte wanted the ground to open up and swallow her. Ross never turned up unexpectedly: he always phoned first to check she was free. It was lovely to see him, but she'd been looking forward to another night alone with Angus.

They sat at the dining table, and the silence when they started to eat was awkward rather than companionable.

Angus went to the kitchen for more water. As soon as he was out of earshot, Charlotte leaned towards Ross. "Ross, it's lovely to see you, but you can't stay over."

Ross had just taken a mouthful of food, so couldn't answer straightaway. "Why not?" he said, as soon as he could speak again. "You aren't up for a night of no-strings passion? You were insatiable a few months ago in the Seychelles. Even with that damned plaster cast that kept getting in the way."

Charlotte smiled at the memory. Ross had flown out to join her. He had been a welcome relief from her frustration over her lack of relationship with Angus – and he had helped her memory of being kidnapped fade a little. But her relationship with Ross had never been anything more than friendship. Though he was a great friend who understood the pressures of being stupidly wealthy, he was too young for her, and most of all, he wasn't Angus. "It's not that, but Angus is staying in the spare room at the moment, and I can't do it while he's in the house. Especially as—"

"Wait ... he's staying here and you aren't sleeping with each other?" Ross's eyes narrowed. "Why's he staying here if you're not an item?"

"There's a World War 2 bomb near his house and he's been evacuated while they defuse it. That's the only reason."

"That must be frustrating. Especially as you have fallen head over heels in love with him. So having sex with another man in the next room isn't your thing?" Ross chuckled.

Charlotte started to regret spilling her heart out to Ross when they were on holiday. They'd both got very drunk one night not long after he'd arrived and she'd told Ross a no-hold's barred description of her feelings for Angus. "No, it's not. Anyway, I thought you were seeing Leticia Chebot-Hamilton. Didn't that work out?"

Ross grimaced. "We went on a couple of dates, but I think she saw me as her pet bit of rough. She went running back to some earl she dated at Cambridge a few years ago."

"Nasty."

"She hardly ate anything, either. Romantic meals were an absolute no-no. She'd sit there with a lettuce leaf and a glass of water."

"You'll just have to go undercover and find a nice woman by pretending you aren't minted. Like that TV programme, Undercover Boss. I know: Undercover Billionaire! You could find your true love while you're working in

Subway or McDonalds." Charlotte's lips twitched and she tried not to laugh at her own joke.

Ross sipped his water. "You've got all the answers, haven't you?"

"Always."

Angus came back with the water jug and the awkward silence resumed.

"Angus, I'd like to thank you," Ross said not long after.

Angus said nothing, but raised his eyebrows.

"You see," Ross continued, "Charlotte has been the happiest I've known her since she started working with you. It's nice to see her so settled."

Angus looked at Charlotte, then back at Ross, utterly confused. "Are you joking?"

"No. I'd never joke about things like that."

Angus nodded. "Charlotte's help has been invaluable. I couldn't do this job without her." He poured more water into Charlotte's glass, then his own.

Ross sat back. "I've tried to get her to work with me multiple times, but she always says no, so I've stopped asking. I don't know what you have that I don't, but the main thing is that she's happy."

Charlotte shot Ross a look. "I could never work for you. Firstly, because I signed a contract when I sold the company that bans me from working in cybersecurity for five years. Secondly because, as a boss, you'd be a complete nightmare. I've seen the people who work for you and they have no life outside work."

Ross smiled. "I pay them more than enough for their lack of social life. Is that your phone ringing somewhere, Char?"

"Yes." She got up to answer it, leaving Ross and Angus alone.

"So, what are you doing in the area, Ross?"

Ross looked up. "I just wanted to give the car a run out. It's been in the garage for too long."

Angus nodded. "It's a Ferrari 296GTB, isn't it?"

"Yeah. You know about supercars?"

"A bit. It's new this year, I think?"

"Yep. I had to give them a huge bribe to get to the front of the queue. It's beautiful to drive, though. I took it to Silverstone a few weeks ago. Finally got some speed up."

"Do you mind if I have a look inside it before you go?"

"Not at all. I'll take you for a run out in it if you like."

Two hours later, Angus and Ross arrived back at Charlotte's house. Ross had driven him to Exmouth then along the coast to Lyme Regis and back, and not for the first time, Angus had wanted a Ferrari himself.

He'd expected Ross to break the speed limit, but he hadn't. The car was just perfect: it didn't need excessive speed to be a pleasure to sit in.

When they returned, Charlotte was back in her office, researching the case. Angus went up to his room, leaving Ross and Charlotte alone downstairs.

Ross was annoyingly nice, and Angus was genuinely starting to like him, but his mood darkened when he thought of him with Charlotte. Ross hadn't driven over for a friendly chat with her. He hadn't just been giving the car a run out. He'd come here for the 'benefit' part of their friendship.

He brooded in his room, but much to his surprise, Charlotte knocked on his door a few minutes later. "Ross has gone," she said. "He said to say goodbye. Did you enjoy the drive?"

Angus didn't try to hide his surprise. He'd expected to see Ross at breakfast and be piggy in the middle. "Er, yes, thanks. He's a nice man." *Annoyingly nice.* He wanted to hate him, but there wasn't anything to dislike except for the fact that he got to have sex with Charlotte.

"He is. We've been friends a while: we have a lot in common. Both of us grew up in dodgy places and have ended up with lots of money. Ross is a billionaire, though, he's got a lot more than me. He made his money from cryptocurrency – got in early when it all kicked off. Anyway, I came up to say that I'm going to carry on researching for a while and then head to bed for an early night. You know where everything is."

Angus watched Charlotte leave his room relieved that Ross wasn't staying the night. He wasn't sure how he would have coped knowing they were at it in the next room.

The next morning, Charlotte went down for breakfast to find Helena batch cooking. She kissed her friend on the cheek, then headed straight for the coffee machine.

"Morning," said Helena. "Sleep vell?"

Charlotte, still in her pyjamas, yawned. "I did, although it took a while to actually get to sleep. My brain was whirling."

"You need step avay from computer screen. All ze blue light it stop sleeping."

The coffee machine joined the conversation as it ground the coffee beans and heated the water.

"I know, Helena, I know. I already have screens that filter blue light, but I need to find a hobby away from a screen." Charlotte leaned against the kitchen counter.

"You need try art or craft. Keep hands busy. Listen to podcast while you do."

"That's not a bad idea, actually. I'll have a think."

Helena took a potato from a plastic bag and started to peel it. "For moment, when you say you no sleep, I thought you and Mr Angus..." She gave Charlotte a very obvious wink.

The coffee machine finished its job. Charlotte picked up her mug and took a sip. "Sadly not."

"He been here two nights and nothing?"

"Ross turned up out of the blue last night."

"Ross? You let him stay night?" Helena stared at her, incredulous.

"God, no. I told him he couldn't stay with Angus here. He was a darling about it, of course, and told me..." She lowered her voice to a whisper. "He told me to just tell Angus how I feel."

"He right about zat." Helena waved the potato peeler.

Charlotte sighed. "Easy for you to say."

"How much longer Mr Angus stay? When zey get rid of bomb?"

"I have no idea. So far, all they've said is that they need to do a controlled explosion and it will be a few days at least."

"Still time, zen!"

"Still time for what?" Angus walked into the kitchen, dressed for the day in dark-grey trousers and a light-grey shirt.

Charlotte and Helena exchanged glances and Charlotte wondered how much of their conversation he'd heard.

"Coffee?" Charlotte asked, and opened the cupboard for a mug.

"Yes, please."

"Sleep well?" Charlotte asked as she pushed the button for an Americano.

"Yes. Still as comfortable as the last time you asked, thank you."

Charlotte noticed Angus's gaze straying to her bright red tartan pyjamas and suddenly felt very self-conscious. The last time he'd seen her in her nightwear was the day they'd met. She should have got dressed before coming down, or at least put a dressing gown on. She waited for the machine to finish, then handed the mug to Angus. "I'll get dressed."

She returned fully clothed and showered as soon as she could to find Angus and Helena chatting as they both chopped and peeled a variety of vegetables. She opened her mouth to tell Angus that he didn't need to help Helena, but they seemed happy cooking together. She felt a pang of jealousy. If she cooked herself, she could be the one bonding over cubed courgettes.

"By the way," she said, "when I was doing my research yesterday evening, I found out that tomorrow night is the rugby club's annual awards dinner. I think we should go and see what we can find out. We'd have to ask Trevor to get us in, but I can't see why he'd object if it's to do with the case."

Angus considered this. "We could – but we'd run the risk of being recognised. I'm not sure it's a good idea."

"We've only been in the club once so far," Charlotte replied. "And I doubt any of them saw us outside James's house. We just need to make sure we don't stand out."

Helena, who had been stirring a large pot of the vegetables on the hob, turned. "Charlotte very beautiful woman. Her blonde hair make her stand out even though she middle-age."

"Middle-aged?" Charlotte repeated in mock disgust. "I suppose I could dye it – not a permanent colour, but I could go brunette for a few days. Or grey – that would definitely make me invisible. Middle-aged women with grey hair are always ignored."

"Zer is one way to be completely invisible at a party like zis." Helena went back to stirring the pot.

"How?" Charlotte asked.

Helena looked over her shoulder and grinned. "Be waitress."

Charlotte gasped. "Yes!" She grabbed Helena's shoulders, turned her round and kissed her on the cheek. "You're a genius. I'll waitress at the event and be able to find out *much* more."

"I can do too," Helena offered. "I vill help listen and watch."

Angus, who was feeling rather left out, gave a small cough. "I'm not sure what you'll find out, but joining the waiting staff is a good way to make sure you aren't spotted. You could try wearing glasses and changing your hairstyle so it's different from usual."

Charlotte smiled. "Don't worry, I'll make sure I look completely different."

"Angus, vill you go to party too?"

"Yes, of course he'll be there." Charlotte turned to Angus. "You will, won't you?"

"We should both be there, but it isn't a good idea for us both to be waiting staff."

"Do you think it's beneath you?" She challenged.

Angus pushed his glasses up his nose. "Of course not. But I feel I'd be much better placed amongst the guests."

"You could be a barman. Lots of people talk at the bar."

"But then I won't be able to keep an eye on where everyone is. There's CCTV in the building. I could watch that."

"So you'll hide yourself away?"

"Not necessarily. If I see something worth leaving the CCTV room for, I'll mingle to try and find out what's going on."

Charlotte clapped her hands and jumped up and down. "Excellent – I'll finally get to see you in black tie!"

Angus went back to chopping carrots. "I'll call Trevor when I finish this and let him know we want to be there tomorrow evening."

After breakfast, Charlotte and Angus worked in Charlotte's office, researching the background of the men who'd visited James. Grigore had gone off to Comm Fab, but phoned an hour later with bad news. "Zey give me application form and tell me come back next veek, ven manager return."

Charlotte screwed her face up. "That's disappointing. What are you doing now?"

"I stay here for while and have coffee in pop-up cafe, zee if Screwball come in."

"That's a good idea. Thanks."

"No problem."

She ended the call and updated Angus, who was writing in his notebook.

He stretched his arms above his head and yawned. "Have you found out much on the men?"

"Yes, a fair bit. Shall we go over what we know?"

"I'll go first." Angus stood up and went to the conspiracy board. "Coach Lee Clarke is known as 'Coach Clarke' to everyone at the club. He's forty-two, and has played amateur rugby all his life with local teams, starting in South Devon where he grew up. He worked as an electrician for the council until eight years ago, when he went to university as a mature student. He did a degree in sports coaching, specialising in rugby. He was taken on by Devon

Rugby four years ago and has been in the same role ever since. He's married to Josie and they have no children.

"Anything interesting on his social media accounts?"

"No. He has Instagram and Twitter accounts but rarely posts, and when he does it's usually holiday pictures. Nothing else."

"It's so annoying when people do that," said Charlotte. "I mean, thinking everyone wants to see your holiday and nothing else."

"That's why I stay away from social media as much as possible," Angus replied.

"What about Oliver Miller?"

"Oliver is twenty six, plays full-back, and came to the club two years ago after transferring from Saracens. He grew up in Norwich and had a love for rugby from school, where he captained the school team. Nothing unusual on his social media. He uses Instagram, mainly, and most of his posts show him and his girlfriend Kaylee, a beautician who works in an Exeter salon. She moved with him when he moved clubs and they live together in a flat at Exeter Quayside." Angus paused and looked at the pictures on the conspiracy board. "I couldn't find anything remotely suspicious about either of them. I also looked for clues to Screwball's real name, but there was nothing."

Charlotte changed places with Angus. "I've been looking into Tom Hunter. He's twenty seven and he's interesting. Unlike most rugby players, who are middle class at least and go to private schools, Tom went to a state school, grew up on a council estate, and is as working class as you can get."

"That is unusual," Angus commented.

"He's proudly working class and has said in many interviews that he was surprised how nice the 'toffs' were."

"So he might have some class issues?"

"I don't think so. He's done several interviews about being a rugby player with a working-class background, and he's an advocate for getting more children from state schools into the game. He's quite active on Twitter and Instagram, usually posting photos of him and his girlfriend walking the dogs."

Angus nodded. "All right. Was there anything on social media that made it look like this bunch were up to anything? Any mention of their meeting?"

Charlotte shook her head. "There's nothing to indicate they socialise outside the club. However, I saw on an unofficial Facebook group that all the players go out drinking occasionally. In their favourite pubs they're usually given a private room, because of groupies."

"Groupies? People still use that word?" Angus said with an amused tone.

"Apparently so."

"Well, we'll just have to find out what was going on some other way. I take it you're planning on hacking their Wi-Fi and all their devices."

"If so, I wouldn't tell you. You always tell me not to mention it."

Angus sighed. "Maybe we'll learn something tomorrow, at the awards."

Chapter Nine

The next day, it hadn't take Charlotte long to get dressed in her waitress's uniform of a black skirt and a white blouse. It brought back memories of her time at university. She'd been virtually penniless, studying for her computer science degree and working two jobs: evenings at a local pizza restaurant and weekends stacking shelves in a supermarket.

Her normally blonde hair was covered with a dark brown wig she'd bought a few months ago in case she ever needed to disguise herself. As she looked at herself in the mirror, Charlotte decided that she quite liked the brunette look.

She tied her hair back in a ponytail, decided on no makeup and found the pair of glasses with plain lenses she'd bought on a whim a while back, just in case.

When she came downstairs, Angus, Helena and Grigore were all waiting in the kitchen. The look of surprise on Angus's face was unmistakable. "Wow, you look completely different."

"Good. I want to make sure no one recognises me."

Then she looked properly at Angus in black tie and her heart almost stopped. "You look very dashing."

"Thank you." He smiled, and they made their way outside to the Bentley.

Once they were all inside the car, Charlotte took three tiny flesh-coloured earpieces from a small bag and held them in her palm. "We need to test these."

Angus eyed them suspiciously. "What are they?"

"Radios, so that we can talk to each other. Don't worry, they're encrypted. No one will be able to tap into them."

Helena took one of the devices and put it in her ear. Angus looked at Charlotte's face, then back at her hand. He sighed, then took one too.

Charlotte put in the remaining earpiece. "OK, can you hear me through it?"

"Yez," Helena said.

Angus nodded.

"Great. Just remember to take it off if you go to the toilet. It has AI to remove background noise, but you never know..." She grinned.

They arrived at the rugby club well before the event was due to begin, so that they could have a word with Trevor beforehand. They found him putting the final touches to the main conference room.

The room looked enchanting, with fifteen huge round tables set for ten people each. Each table had a multi-level tealight holder with ten lights. The tables were set with silver cutlery on white tablecloths, and a magnum of champagne in an ice bucket waited for the guests. The stage at the front was decorated with various banners showing in-action photos of the team and behind-the-scenes staff. A seating plan was displayed at the entrance.

Angus and Charlotte walked towards Trevor, who was

talking to a female member of staff. He acknowledged them with a nod, sent away the employee, and came over. He shook Angus's hand, but didn't seem to recognise Charlotte. "Hello. I'm not sure why you're here, but if it helps find the troll, it's fine."

Angus released Trevor's hand. "Don't worry, we'll make sure no one knows we're here."

Trevor glanced at Charlotte again, looking faintly puzzled. "Security have been told to give you complete access to the CCTV, as you asked."

"Thank you."

A loud bang came from the stage. They all turned to see the woman Trevor had been talking to had knocked over a banner.

"Excuse me." Trevor rolled his eyes and headed for the stage.

Angus turned to Charlotte. "I'll see you later."

Charlotte nodded and made her way to the kitchens.

Angus returned to the club's reception, and the security guard on the door, whose name badge read '*Nigel*', showed him to the CCTV room.

The room had a desk facing a bank of screens, all showing a different pictures from the cameras around the club. Sitting at the desk was another security guard.

"The CCTV room is staffed all the time," said Nigel. "This is Rob, who's on night shift tonight." Rob turned to Angus and nodded, then swivelled back to the screens. "Mr Holland said I was to give you access to everything," said Nigel, giving Angus a searching look. "Want to tell me what it's about, so me and Rob can keep an eye out?"

Angus pushed his glasses up his nose. "I'm sorry, but I

can't tell you just now. Mr Holland's instructions are that it has to remains need to know, but thanks anyway."

Nigel shrugged "No skin off my nose," and he carried on watching. Rob showed no reaction.

"Is there a chair I can use?" Angus asked.

"Yeah." Nigel left the room and came back with a plastic chair. It didn't look very comfortable, but Angus took it and sat down. He checked which location each screen was filming. The top ones were in and around the pitch. Three showed the car park, one the main entrance outside, and one was located just inside.

The other screens showed the conference areas: mostly the corridors, with one pointing to the stage and another two around the conference room.

Angus pushed the device further into his ear. "I can't hear either of you," he murmured.

There was a crackle, then he heard Charlotte's voice. "These things have a range of two hundred metres, but I haven't been talking because I've had a know-it-all supervisors giving me my orders. I'll be handing out drinks and then canapés before the meal, then serving the meal itself."

Helena cut in. "As soon as he hear my Romanian accent, he give me dirty look."

"So disgusting," said Charlotte.

"I'm in the CCTV room," Angus told them.

Rob glanced at him. "You talking to yourself?"

"No." Angus pointed to his ear.

"Earpiece, huh?" Rob rolled his shoulders. "Must be serious if there's more than one of you. Go on, tell me what you're looking for. Maybe I can help."

Angus eyed Rob. The buttons on his shirt were straining over his paunch, and his expression didn't inspire Angus with confidence as to his abilities. He wasn't necessarily a bad security guard, but Angus didn't think he'd be an asset to their investigation.

"Thanks for the offer," he replied. "If I see anything I need you to keep an eye on, I'll let you know."

Charlotte stood near the entrance to the conference room with a tray of wine glasses, looking over the throng of the guests. Most of the guests had arrived and their rising chatter made Charlotte anxious. Noisy rooms like this stressed her out. If she'd been a guest, she would have sought sanctuary outside or in the ladies' loos.

The wives and girlfriends all seemed to know each other, and air kissed when they met anyone they knew.

Angus had informed her when Oliver, Tom and Coach Clarke arrived with their partners. However, almost as soon as they entered the room they, like the rest of the players and staff, were taken away to schmooze pompous-looking people in suits. *Probably sponsors and local dignitaries*, thought Charlotte.

Then Charlotte caught sight of someone who made her do a double-take. Her heart missed a beat and she closed her eyes for a moment. "Oh, for god's sake," she muttered.

"What is it?" Angus murmured in her earpiece.

"You'll never believe who's here. Angus, you should have warned me. Unless you didn't see?"

"Not Idris?" said Helena. "That bastard ex of yours, he get everywhere."

"No. *Much* worse. It's Angus's ex-wife, Rhona." She'd only met Rhona a few times, but whenever she did, there was hate on both sides.

Rhona was dressed in a floor-length dark-green velvet dress. She had her hair up and was wearing a full face of make-up. *She looks like a fancy cucumber*, thought Charlotte, and smirked.

"Yes, I saw her arrive," said Angus.

"You could have warned me!" Charlotte whispered angrily.

"I thought it best not to. She's probably been invited because she's a councillor."

"All right for some," said Charlotte, her nose in the air.

Rhona stood with a glass of red wine in her hand, chatting with a group of five other people. Charlotte didn't recognise any of them.

"Be nice," Helena said, a warning note in her voice, but Charlotte didn't reply. She was busy trying not to think of accidentally-on-purpose spilling a drink over her, treading on her dress, or maybe even attaching a piece of toilet roll to the back of her dress. Then she took a deep breath and composed herself. She was above doing such childish things, but it was fun to think about it.

She headed to the bar, leaving her drinks tray at the end, and collected a tray of canapés. That would enable her to mingle with the crowd and listen to their conversations.

First, she headed for Oliver Miller. Unlike the other attendees at James's house, who were now talking to sponsors, Oliver Miller was talking to Coach Clarke. They were at the side of the room, heads close together, watching the throng. Charlotte offered canapés but they turned them down. She took up position nearby to try and catch some of their conversation, but the background noise blocked out what they were saying. It was most frustrating.

She was looking around the room for another target, when Angus's voice came over her earpiece. "The mystery man has just arrived. Screwball's here."

"What, really?" Charlotte glanced towards the door.

"Yes, he's just coming in."

"So he's on the guest list," Charlotte said. "I'm coming down," said Angus. "I'll try to get close to him. Follow him, if I need to."

Charlotte could have sighed with relief. "Watch out for your ex-wife," she said.

"Excuse me?" said Angus.

Charlotte smiled. "You might want to warn her you're at work."

"Oh. Yes, I will."

Chapter Ten

Angus entered the room and spotted Screwball straight away. He was dressed in black tie, just like everyone else, but there was something shabby about him. Angus couldn't put his finger on what, but he didn't fit in.

What he also noticed was that anyone whom Screwball spoke to instantly tensed up.

Screwball took a glass of wine from the nearest tray and stopped a waitress going by for some canapés. He ate them one after the other, popping them in his mouth and chewing like a gorilla.

He wandered through the crowd for a while, looking for someone. He saw Tom Hunter, schmoozing with a small group of people and caught his eye then strolled towards him.

Angus meandered over and stood close enough to listen in. He took out his phone and pretended to look through emails.

"What are you doing here?" Tom muttered, frowning. "You weren't invited."

"Now, now. I came to keep an eye on you all." Screwball swigged half his glass of wine then surveyed the room. "Nice do."

Charlotte circulated with her tray of canapés, moving past the tables, till she reached the pair. She stopped and offered the tray.

Screwball took three, stacked them on top of each other, and threw them in his mouth.

"They'll do. Give us some more, love," he said. Charlotte held out the tray and he helped himself, chewing with his mouth open and gulping them down. Charlotte glanced at Angus, who tilted his head and looked away, and she moved on.

When Screwball had swallowed the last of his canapés he drained his wine glass, then looked at it. "Not bad plonk, that. Bit tart." He laughed.

"It's not plonk," snapped Tom.

"Prefer whisky, myself."

"You know you can't stay. There's nowhere for you to sit. There's a seating plan; it's all arranged."

"I'm sure you can find me a seat, mate. If not, I'll have your spot. I'd like to get to know your girlfriend properly. You've not introduced us yet." Screwball spoke in a matter-of-fact tone, but his smile said that he wouldn't take no for an answer. "Get me near the others. I want to check they're behaving themselves, too."

Tom stared at him, his frown depending to a scowl. Screwball watched the room, his expression noncommittal. "Now you listen, Tom. If you hurt me, you're only hurting yourself. Or your lovely girlfriend."

Tom had a panicked look in his eye. "I'll see what I can do." He stalked off. Angus kept looking forward, in the hope that Screwball would think he was security. After all, it was partly true.

He studied the throng of people having a good time. The noise in the room was increasing as people drank more alcohol. A few of the men who had visited James's house glanced at Screwball, but none came over to talk to him. That spoke volumes.

Angus was torn between staying to keep an eye on Screwball, or returning to the CCTV room. It looked like everybody was giving Screwball a wide berth. But then he spotted James Finley, the man who'd been sending the threatening messages. He was talking to a small group of people, none of whom Angus recognised. He had a half-empty pint of beer in his hand and a smile on his face. There was a loud guffaw from the group, as if someone had told a joke.

Angus spoke quietly through the earpiece. "James Finley is also here. Near the bar area."

There was a pause, then Charlotte spoke. "Shit. Really? What's he doing here? Can you find out why he's been invited?"

"I'll try. I'm going to stay here for now, but I'll have to make myself scarce if he comes near, in case he recognises me."

"Well," said Charlotte, "I guess it's more important to know what they're up to than why he's here."

They were interrupted by a whine from the sound system, followed by Trevor announcing that everyone should take their seats as dinner was about to be served.

Everyone found their place and sat down. Tom went over to Screwball and directed him to a table at the back. Angus didn't recognise anyone else at that table, but he watched Screwball introduce himself and sit down.

Angus looked around the room and noted where everyone of interest to him was sitting. Then he stood near the back to blend in. They were each at different tables, and it would be impossible to find out what they were all talking about. Maybe Charlotte would be able to overhear something.

At least they would be able to follow Screwball home and find out more about who he was. Angus texted Grigore and asked him to be ready, in case Screwball left before the party finished.

Just as Angus put his phone away he heard a familiar voice. "Hello, stranger." It was Rhona, his ex-wife.

Angus looked up and smiled at her. "Hello, yourself. You look lovely."

"Flattery will get you everywhere. What are you doing here? You're the last person I'd expect to see at an event like this." Her eyes narrowed. "In fact, from the way you're looking at everybody you look more as if you're here working."

"Well, Rhona," he said, for the sake of Charlotte and Helena, "I *am* here working. If you can keep that to yourself, I'd be grateful."

Rhona tapped the side of her nose, then looked around the room. "Where's your blonde bit? Not here in a designer ballgown?"

"She isn't. And she's not my blonde bit. I'll thank you to stop calling her that."

He heard Charlotte groan in his earpiece. "God, she still calls me that? How insufferable."

Rhona didn't reply to Angus's request. Judging by her flushed cheeks, she'd had a fair bit to drink.

He decided to change the subject. "Any news on when the bomb will be disarmed?"

Rhona's shoulders pulled back and she switched into councillor mode. "They're working as fast as they can. It should only be a few more days."

Angus nodded. "Shouldn't you get back to the meal?" he asked. "The starters are coming out."

"Are you trying to get rid of me?" She made a mock-hurt face at him.

"Not at all, but I wouldn't want you to miss out on the pigeon and pork belly terrine."

"Urgh, disgusting," Helena said, through the earpiece. "Pigeon is sky rat."

"Adios, Angus. See you later." Rhona walked back to her table.

Angus decided to go back to the CCTV room while the meal progressed. A three-course meal would take some time. When he got in the room, Rob nodded at him. "Not found what you were looking for?"

"Not yet." Angus sat in the same chair as before and stared at the screens. Nigel glanced at him but said nothing.

It didn't take long for Angus to find himself looking out for Charlotte on the screen. He spotted her several times carrying plates and drinks. She looked so different in her brunette wig and waitress outfit.

When the desserts had been served, Trevor came onstage and gave a speech and then handed out awards. Best coach, best players, best try of the season and a special award for best effort. Once that was over, the disco started.

It took a few songs for anyone to get on the dance floor, but once a few people had braved it, the floor started to fill. Angus decided to leave the CCTV room and go back in to see if he could overhear anything. Then Charlotte spoke in his ear. "Oliver and Tom have just gone out through a side door. I'm going to follow and try to eavesdrop."

"Won't they see you?"

"If they do, I'll say I'm having a break."

"I'll come too. Where is it?"

"Past the bar, then down the stairs and outside. I'm heading out now."

Thirty seconds later, Angus ran downstairs, his heart thumping at the excitement to where Charlotte was waiting. She opened the door and they went outside.

Chapter Eleven

Outside, the patio area was empty. However, voices could be heard round the corner of the building. Angus edged as close to the corner as he could, followed by Charlotte, their backs pressed against the wall.

"We can't blab," one of them said. "If we do, they'll kill us. They're always threatening my girlfriend too."

"They can't kill all of us," said the other man.

"Well, they'll make us pay, then," said the first man. "They'll make sure we never play another match. You know that story in the paper a while ago? The man whose thumb got cut off in an accident? That was no accident."

"How do you know?"

"He told me. He'd been involved with Screwball for a while and somehow, he put his foot in it. We'll just have to do what they ask."

"But if we do, they'll just keep on at us. There'll be no end to it."

"What choice have we got? I'm not risking me or my girlfriend. Sorry, but I ain't."

Just as the man stopped speaking, Charlotte's phone beeped loudly. "Shit!" she mouthed. She'd turned the sound up to hear it better in the conference room.

"Did you hear that?" one of them said. "Someone's round the corner. They might be listening..."

Charlotte and Angus stared at each other, fear of being caught on both their faces. Then Charlotte acted on instinct. She stepped in in front of Angus, pushed herself against him, then grabbed his arms and wrapped them round her. Then she cupped his face in her hands and kissed him.

It took Angus a moment to respond to Charlotte's kiss, but he did. He couldn't stop himself.

Then a man's voice shouted, "Who's there?"

Angus managed a sidelong glance and saw a tall, broad figure inches away, fists clenched. Then he stepped back. "Oh, sorry..."

Charlotte eventually stopped kissing him, and glared at the man, it was Oliver Miller.

Tom appeared and frowned at the sight of Angus and Charlotte. "Do you mind?" Charlotte said in a clipped voice. "I'm on my break, and we don't have long." She leaned in for another kiss.

"Er, sorry," said Tom, and they headed to the door. "We'll leave you to it," he added, with a snigger.

As the pair reached the door, it opened. Oliver Miller said, "Not sure it's a good idea to go out there..."

Angus glanced towards the door to see who had come out. It was Rhona, followed by her boyfriend, Malcolm.

"Thought you said you were working," she said to Angus, and amused expression on her face. "It's not like you to put on such a public display of affection. Won't your blonde bit be upset that you're out here with someone else?"

Charlotte narrowed her eyes, then reluctantly let go of Angus and turned towards Rhona. "I am the blonde bit."

Rhona raised her eyebrows, then looked Charlotte up and down. "Are you working as a waitress here?"

"Part-time job," said Charlotte. "Nothing wrong with that." She put her hands on her hips, challenging Rhona, the Labour Party councillor, to demean someone working as a server.

Then realisation dawned on Rhona's face. "You're here on a case, aren't you? Mum's the word." She mimed zipping her mouth shut. "You could at least try to keep your hands off each other when you're at work, though. As for you, Angus, I thought you'd have better self-control. Come on Malcolm, you can smoke over there." She beckoned to Malcolm, and they disappeared round the corner.

When Rhona and Malcolm had gone, Charlotte flopped against the wall and sighed with relief. "That was lucky. Oldest trick in the book: pretend you're getting off with someone and you can get away with anything. Shame we didn't get to hear more, though. Anyway, from what they were saying, I think they're being blackmailed. Do you agree?"

Angus hardly heard a word she said. All he could think about was that Charlotte had kissed him and he'd really, really liked it. Especially the bit where she'd pressed herself against him. He gave himself a mental shake. *Concentrate on the job in hand, man.*

He was about to reply when Helena spoke in his earpiece. "You need come up, there problem in men's toilets."

"I'm on my way," said Angus. He headed for the door, and ran upstairs, with Charlotte right behind him.

Angus and Charlotte hurried through the conference room, which took quite a long time, as people were now milling around or on the dance floor.

Angus spotted Helena standing in the corridor outside the entrance to the men's toilets. Nigel, the security man, was by the door stopping any men from going in. He caught sight of Angus and jerked his chin up. "Trevor's in there. We think Coach Clarke has locked himself in a cubicle."

Angus went in to find Trevor knocking on the door of one of the cubicles. "What's happened?" he asked Trevor, then realised that Charlotte had followed him in.

"Coach Clarke is in there and he's not answering," Trevor replied, worry etched on his face.

Angus stepped back and inspected the door. The bottom was flush with the floor, but there was a gap at the top. He went into the next cubicle, stood on the toilet seat and looked over. Coach Clarke was sitting on the closed toilet seat, fully clothed, his head against the side wall of the cubicle.

"I can see him: he's unconscious," Angus said. He suspected the man might be dead, but he didn't want to alarm them until he knew for sure. He jumped down from the toilet seat. "We need to break the door down. Charlotte, call an ambulance."

She pulled out her phone and Angus shoulder-barged the cubicle door. It didn't move. He tried again, and it shifted a little. He barged it once more and it banged open, the lock on the inside dangling.

Coach Clarke hadn't moved an inch, and his eyes were

still shut. Angus felt his neck for a pulse, but he already knew the answer.

Charlotte put her hands to her head. "Oh my goodness, is he dead?"

Angus nodded. "I'm afraid so. I'll call the police. Trevor, this could be a crime scene. Until we know what's happened, we need to make sure it isn't contaminated. Keep everyone out."

Trevor nodded, then sighed. "This is going to be a PR nightmare," Shaking his head, he left the bathroom and they heard him talking to Nigel.

Angus scanned the cubicle and the body for clues. "He doesn't have any visible wounds..." Then he spotted a small silver canister, like a silver bullet on the floor. He took a photo of it with his phone, then realised Charlotte was doing the same with her phone.

Angus pointed. "That canister... that's often used for recreational drug taking."

"What sort of drugs?" asked Charlotte.

"Entonox, usually: nitrous oxide, or laughing gas."

"Well, I can understand that. It was brilliant when I was giving birth. That stuff won't kill you though, will it?"

"It shouldn't. But it could be a number of other drugs. The police will have to analyse it."

Quickly, Angus took photos of the rest of the room. Once the police arrived, they wouldn't want him there.

A few minutes later, Charlotte and Angus watched from the foyer as the police entered the building. Two uniformed officers and one in plain clothes.

Oh, God, thought Charlotte. It was that horrible sergeant again. The one who used to work for Angus. The one who had accused her of kidnapping her ex-husband. She'd disliked him the moment she set eyes on him. She stepped behind Angus and hoped the sergeant wouldn't see her. That probably wouldn't help, though, as they'd ask for a list of everyone at the party. Not that she'd help. What a great night it was turning out to be. First Angus's ex-wife, and now *him.* And she wasn't about to change her opinion thank you very much. She was like Mr Darcy from *Pride and Prejudice*: her good opinion, once lost, was lost forever.

She wished her brother Mark was investigating instead, but he was far too busy these days working on gang crime.

Charlotte murmured to Angus, "It's that horrible sergeant of yours. The one who thought I'd kidnapped Idris."

Angus turned to her. "He's not horrible, and we've been over this quite a few times. As Idris's ex-wife, it was due process to eliminate you from their enquiries."

Charlotte knew he was right, but that didn't make it any better. "*It was due process to eliminate you from their enquiries,*" she said, in a sing-song tone. "You sound like such a policeman when you say things like that."

Angus rolled his eyes, then stepped forward to speak to Simon.

Charlotte decided to leave him to it and went on the hunt for Helena. She found her in the main conference room, clearing away dishes and glasses, the disco music was still blaring out, with lots of people completely oblivious to what had been happening elsewhere. "You don't have to do that any more," she said, looking at Helena's pile of crockery. "The coach is dead. They found him in a toilet cubicle." Charlotte shouted into Helena's ear.

"Dead?" Helena mouthed back.

"Yep. Not sure if it was murder or not, but it looks like a drug overdose."

Helena tutted. "Vhy people take drugs. It zo stupid."

Charlotte nodded. "I know. Angus is talking to the police now."

The loud music playing in the background suddenly stopped and Trevor walked onstage. He tapped the microphone a couple of times, then spoke. "Er, look, everyone, there's been a terrible discovery and we're ending the evening early. I'm very sorry, but I must ask you all to register your name and address with the police and then go home. There are some officers by the entrance who will take your details."

A loud groan rose up and everyone started talking to each other. Then someone shouted, "What happened? Did someone die?"

"I can't talk about it," said Trevor. "I know it's a shame to stop the event, but I wouldn't unless it was absolutely necessary."

Charlotte wasn't sure it was necessary. Most of the people there were oblivious, and very, very drunk.

"I get rid of plates and ve go?" asked Helena.

"You get Grigore to take you home. I'll stay and come back later with Angus."

Helena walked towards the kitchens with the plates and Charlotte headed for the CCTV room. She found it empty and took out a flash drive, plugged it into the main computer, and downloaded the last few hours of footage. Then she went to look for Angus.

She found him in the corridor near the toilet, talking to his old sergeant, and decided not to disturb them. She hung around in the shadows and watched as people left. She couldn't see Tom, Oliver, or James there. She wandered around the main areas in case she'd missed them, but it seemed they'd all gone home.

"Oi, you!" It was the catering manager, looking at her accusingly over a stack of chairs. "You're supposed to be helping clear up in the main hall. Where have you been? I haven't seen you since the dessert went out."

Charlotte pondered her response. She could tell the truth, of course, but it would be better to remain incognito in the coming days or weeks. "Sorry, I have to go home now," she said.

He shook his head. "You won't get your full pay if you leave now. Honestly, why can't I get the staff to work a full night? Not like the old days. Well, on your own head be it."

"I was volunteering anyway," she retorted as he walked away.

Grigore and Helena were waiting for them in the Bentley. Angus was exhausted but Charlotte was very alert. "Tell me what your old sergeant said," she demanded, the moment Grigore pulled away.

"Not much. They suspect a drug overdose but they're keeping an open mind. The canister points to that, but they won't know for sure until the autopsy."

"How long will that take?"

"A few days. And even then, he could have brought the canister there himself."

"Was he known to be a drug taker?"

"I don't know. We'll need to speak to his wife and friends," Angus yawned.

"We can do that in the morning." Charlotte looked out of the window at the passing cars. "You know it's been so many years since I was a waitress, I thought I'd forgotten how to balance carrying lots of plates but it was just like riding a bike, it all came back to me. I quite enjoyed it. Except for the rude drunk people."

"Who was rude to you?" Angus asked.

"A couple of people. One seemed to think it was my job to fetch drinks for him at the bar. I ignored him at first, then he had a go at me for not bringing the drink, so I purposefully brought the wrong one." Her shoulders shook as she chuckled about it.

"Then when he protested that I'd brought him a whiskey and coke instead of a pint of lager I told him he'd definitely asked for the whiskey and coke, except I didn't tell him it was just a coke. I told him it was on me, and he seemed to like that."

"Mind games. I like it." Helena commented.

"I hoped it might sober him up a bit. He'd been downing pints like there was no tomorrow."

The next morning, Angus came downstairs for breakfast and found Charlotte already up and dressed. "I've just spoken to Trevor," he said. "He's given us permission to interview any of the team or coaches to help with the police investigation."

"That's good." Charlotte held up her phone. "I'm watching the CCTV footage from last night. I'm tracking Coach Clarke to see if I can spot him getting drugs from anyone."

"I don't think you'll find anything. If Coach Clarke was looking to buy some drugs, he'd know where all the cameras were and how to avoid them."

Charlotte pondered for a moment. "You're probably right, but I'll check anyway, I might spot something else."

Angus's phone rang. The screen said it was Simon, his ex-sergeant. He pressed *Accept*.

"Simon. Any news?"

"It was murder. The preliminary examination of the body shows organ failure from chloroethane."

"What's that?"

"It's a recreational drug and quite common, but in very diluted amounts. It's found in all sorts of things, from dye to petrol. The capsule was analysed overnight and shows a super-high concentrate of it. That's both unusual and deliberate. It strongly suggests that someone wanted him out of the way. I'll need all the info you gathered last night – this is now a murder enquiry."

Angus sat down. "Do you want me to come over?" asked Simon. "It might be quicker to brief you."

Angus glanced at Charlotte. "I'm at Charlotte's at the moment. My house is inside the bomb zone."

"Unlucky. Come to the station when you can then."

The call ended and Angus relayed the information to Charlotte.

"So he was murdered. Oh my God, that's awful." She stared at the computer screen, processing it. "I'll carry on checking the CCTV footage, then, and see what I can find."

"How exactly did you get hold of it?" Angus asked.

"I went to the CCTV room and downloaded it when you were talking to Simon last night."

"Well, at least we have permission and you didn't have to do any hacking."

Charlotte smiled at him. "Remember that first visit, when Daniel from IT downloaded the troll data? I gave him a USB flash drive to copy it to, but on the drive was a worm virus I wrote." Angus grimaced, but said nothing. "It sits on their network, monitoring everything, and tells me about anything significant." She snorted. "He's not much of a digital security manager if he doesn't check a flash drive. I mean, that's day one, lesson one of cybersecurity training: Never, ever, plug in a flash drive unless it's onto a virtual machine. It's been embedded on their network and they haven't even seen it."

"I don't want to know, remember? How many times do I need to say it?"

"Sorry. Anyway, if we need any info from their computer systems, I have a way in."

"Let's hope we don't. Now, do you need any help looking at the CCTV footage?"

"Yes please, there are so many cameras, and I could do with a second pair of eyes."

Two hours later, they'd scanned most of the footage and hardly seen Coach Clarke at all.

Angus sat back and rubbed his neck, then consulted his notepad. "All I found was Coach Clarke talking to various people, getting a round of drinks, and sitting down to dinner."

"Who was he sitting next to?" Charlotte asked.

"His wife on one side and Martin Hall on the other. He's one of the sponsors."

"I didn't see him on any of the footage I watched. However, I did see two lovebirds having a passionate moment." She turned her screen round and paused the video.

"Wow, Matt Hancock has nothing on him." He met Charlotte's eyes. "Which reminds me – we should talk about you kissing me last night."

Charlotte blinked twice. "Yes – er, sorry about that. It was the only thing I could think of to get us out of rather a sticky situation."

Angus stared at her and she laughed. "You're not going to sue me for sexual harassment, are you? I mean, I don't even have a contract." She smiled at him, then turned her screen back round and began typing.

So it had only been a ploy to get them out of trouble. Of course. He knew that. Angus cleared his throat and pushed his glasses up his nose. The memory of that kiss had been distracting him ever since it happened. Charlotte, he now knew, was a very good kisser. Of course she was. There wasn't much she was bad at.

He decided to do what any other man would, and change the subject. He stood up. "I'll call Trevor. I want to talk to Oliver and Tom about what they saw last night." He headed for the garden. Fresh air would clear his head – and give him some distance from Charlotte. He needed to focus on the case.

Chapter Twelve

A few hours later, Charlotte and Angus were in Teignmouth, parked up on the promenade. A cool wind blew from the east.

Charlotte took out a hairband and tied her hair back. "I've always loved Teignmouth," she said, closing her eyes for a moment. "The beach seems to go on for ever."

"It is lovely," Angus said. "Although the tourists are really annoying in the summer."

"Where are the players training?"

"Just over there." Angus pointed west. A group of about ten men were playing beach volleyball, with about the same number looking on.

"Did Trevor warn them that we were coming?" asked Charlotte.

"He said he'd phone the head coach."

Charlotte frowned. "Don't you think it's strange that they're out training the day after one of their coaches was murdered?"

Angus turned to her. "They don't know he was murdered. Not yet."

"That's true. But he died yesterday, it just seems disrespectful, that's what I mean. Shall we go?"

They headed for the group, and as they approached saw the now-familiar faces of most of the team and the coaches. They stopped just behind the coaches and watched.

The players were dressed in tracksuits with the team logo on the front. The game was energetic, and they watched for several minutes.

"Do you think one of the players killed him?" Charlotte whispered. "I mean, look at their faces. They're all so young and happy, even though one of their coaches has died."

"We need to get one of the group from James's house to tell us why they were meeting that day, and who Screwball is."

"Have you told Simon about Screwball?"

"Not yet. I will when I meet him later."

"Maybe we can get one of the players to tell us."

When the volleyball game finished, Angus walked over to the nearest coach with Charlotte behind him.

"Coach Smith, I'm Angus Darrow. Trevor has contacted you this morning about me talking to the players."

Coach Smith nodded. He was in his fifties, dressed in black tracksuit trousers and a green T-shirt. "Yeah, he did." He glanced at the players, who were taking a break, drinking from water bottles and larking about.

"We need to speak to Oliver Miller and Tom Hunter. Is there somewhere nearby where I can take them?"

Coach Smith eyed Angus warily, and glanced at Charlotte. "We go to the beach cafe over there after training, but we've still got circuits to do. It'll be at least an hour before we've finished." He pointed at a cafe a short distance along the esplanade.

"We need to speak to them urgently: Trevor's orders,"

said Angus. "Please send Oliver first, then send Tom when Oliver returns."

"What's this about, anyway? Trevor never said they could miss training." Coach Smith looked querulous. "They need to take their minds off what happened to Lee. Why can't you wait?"

"I need to speak to them alone, not in a group." Angus pushed his glasses up his nose and gave him a hard stare.

Coach Smith sighed, then turned to the players. "Oliver, come here a minute," he shouted.

Oliver was chatting to another player and looked up when his name was called. He jogged over. "Yeah?"

"This is Angus Darrow. Trevor wants you to talk to him."

Oliver glanced at Angus. "What's up?"

Angus pointed to the beach cafe. "I'll tell you over there."

Chapter Thirteen

The beach cafe was a haven from the insistent wind. It was in need of updating, and had a greasy-spoon feel. The chairs and tables were bolted to the black and white checked floor. It was a shame: the cafe looked out over the beach, and the large windows would have given a breathtaking view of the English Channel if they were clean.

The cafe was deserted except for a woman at the far end, looking at her phone and gently pushing a pram back and forth.

"What would you like?" Angus asked.

"Tea," said Oliver.

Angus went to order, including a coffee for Charlotte.

"Shall we sit here?" Charlotte sat down at a table by one of the windows. Oliver sat opposite, squeezing his bulk into the small fixed space.

Charlotte smiled at him. "Quite windy here. Do you train on the beach a lot?"

"Yeah. Not in the deep winter, but most of the year. We like the change of scene and the volleyball."

Angus arrived with a tray of drinks shortly afterwards.

"Thanks," said Oliver, as Angus put the cup of tea in from of him. "Have we met?"

Angus sat down beside Charlotte and adjusted his tie. "Not properly."

"I remember you two," Oliver said. "You were at the party last night – or rather, outside it. Snogging around the corner." He grinned.

Charlotte wrinkled her nose at the word *snogging*. She gave Angus a sidelong glance. He'd flushed a little.

Oliver leaned forward. "Who are you, anyway, and why do you need to talk to me?" He reached for the sugar sifter.

"We're private investigators," said Angus. "Trevor hired us. We need to talk to you about Coach Clarke."

"Private investigators? If your work involves snogging at parties, it's a great job." He put four sugars in his tea and stirred it.

Angus sighed and took out his notebook and pen.

"We're looking into something for Trevor," said Charlotte. "It involves Coach Clarke."

Oliver's grin disappeared. "I can't believe he's dead."

Angus opened his notebook. "We need you to tell us why you, Tom, Coach Clarke and someone called Screwball met at James Finley's house a few days ago."

Oliver's spoon stopped dead in his tea. "How do you know about that?"

"That doesn't matter."

"Have you been following me?" Oliver stared at Angus. For a moment, Charlotte thought he might grab Angus and throw him across the room. He was big enough to try it.

"We haven't been following you," she said in a reassuring tone, "but we do know you've been meeting up."

"How do you know about the Wednesday Night Club?" There was a look of panic on Oliver's face.

Charlotte tried not to react to this new information. Angus, she could see, already had his poker face in place. "Why don't you tell us all about it, Oliver," he said. "That way, Trevor won't be annoyed."

"Trevor?" Oliver let out a contemptuous huff. "He won't care about us meeting: it's the gambling he won't like. That was Tom's idea. We just met for drinks, and..." He glanced at Charlotte. "Sometimes, we'd watch films or play Grand Theft Auto."

"Anything else?" asked Angus

"We'd play poker, or other card games. Occasionally we'd go to the casino in Plymouth, but not often."

"Other than you, Coach Clarke, Tom Hunter and Screwball, who else went to this club?"

He sat back and crossed his arms. "I'm not telling you any more."

Angus studied Oliver. Charlotte took a sip of coffee, watching Angus gauge what to ask next. She was sure Angus was by no means finished with Oliver.

"What's Screwball's real name?"

"I ain't saying." Oliver gulped down the rest of his tea. The cup looked tiny in his large hand.

"So where does James come in?"

Oliver shrugged. "He's a friend of Tom's."

"Why did you all meet on Wednesday afternoon, it wasn't a normal meeting was it?"

Oliver looked at the table. "We were arranging the next meeting."

Angus sat back. "That's not true. You arranged every other meeting in your WhatsApp group."

Oliver's eyes narrowed. "How do you know that?"

Angus stayed silent. Charlotte had been surprised at that, too, but decided it was a lucky guess on Angus's part.

Angus met Oliver's eyes. "So why were you meeting?"

Oliver glanced out of the window, then shrugged again. "Just wanted to catch up, you know. Like friends do."

The two men stared at each other. Angus broke the silence. "What was Coach Clarke's involvement in the Wednesday Night Club?"

"He just came along. He liked being one of the lads."

"Do you know who was selling him recreational drugs?"

Oliver's gaze found the window again. "Coach Clarke didn't do drugs. Not much, anyway – just the occasional upper. He got stressed now and again."

"How did he get them?"

"I dunno. I don't do anything like that. Never have. I get tested every couple of months and it would show up."

Angus put his pen down. "All right, Oliver, thanks for your time. Would you send Tom over to us, please."

"Er, OK." Oliver slid out from the table and walked away, looking back at them just as he left the cafe.

When he had gone, Charlotte turned to Angus. "Wow, you're so good at that."

Angus gazed out of the window, watching Oliver return to the group. "I got a fair amount out of him but he was hiding more than he told us."

"So they're meeting on Wednesday nights to gamble and play games. It's not exactly something to keep a secret. Do you think someone's blackmailing them, because if they are, I can't see why?"

Angus considered her question. "It's possible they've not told us everything they do. But gambling and playing console games aren't illegal and the club doesn't try to present their players as perfect role models. I mean, most people wouldn't be surprised to find out that men in their twenties or thirties are doing both those things, especially the gaming."

Charlotte shifted in her seat. "There must be something else. And I don't think it's coincidence that two non-club members are involved." She smiled at Angus. "You'll have to work your magic questioning Tom."

Angus nodded. "I'll do my best."

After ten minutes, Tom Hunter still hadn't appeared. Angus walked to the far side of the cafe and looked out of the window. Where the team had been training was an empty beach.

He closed his eyes and sighed. He should have seen it coming. Oliver would have told Tom about their meeting in the cafe.

He headed back to Charlotte. "They've run." He didn't bother to sit down.

"Run? Dammit," said Charlotte. "That means they've definitely got something to hide."

"If we're quick, we can catch them on the road back. They came in a couple of minibuses."

They headed outside just as both minibuses drove past them. "There's Oliver, sitting next to Tom," Charlotte said, pointing. "Stupid bastard."

They ran to Angus's car, got in, and drove towards Exeter.

Chapter Fourteen

They caught up with the minibuses as they pulled into the rugby club car park. Angus had spent the journey berating himself for his lack of foresight, but he pushed his anger aside the moment he stopped the engine and got out of the car.

Oliver was just getting off the minibus, with Tom behind him. Angus didn't say anything to Oliver – it was pointless now – but stopped Tom as soon as he had left the vehicle. "I need to speak to you."

Tom stared at him. "And you are?"

Angus raised his eyebrows. "I'm sure Oliver has told you all about me. We need to talk, and it needs to be now."

"Sorry, I can't. I've got to get to work."

Angus drew himself up. "Tough."

Tom laughed. "You gonna try and stop me?' He puffed his chest out. They both knew that, given his size and stature, he would have no problem harming Angus.

A couple of the other players came over. "You all right, Tom?" one of them said. "Is this dude bothering you?"

Tom laughed. "Nah, mate, I can handle it." He stared at Angus, his face inches away.

Angus put his hands in his pockets. "We can talk now, or we can do it in front of Trevor, after I tell him that you haven't been co-operating."

That made Tom's left eye twitch. "Trevor?"

"Yes, Trevor. I'm working for him, and he wants everyone to help with the investigation. If you have a problem with that, talk to him."

Tom walked away from the others, then gestured to Angus to come over. "Look, I don't have anything to say about the Wednesday Night Club," he muttered. "Even if I wanted to tell you, I couldn't. It would be suicide."

"So you're going to keep quiet?"

"Yes." He stared into the distance, his mouth a firm line.

"Thanks for nothing," said Angus, and walked away.

Charlotte had been standing next to one of the minibuses, watching. Angus saw her and went over. "I take it he was still uncooperative," she said, noting his stern expression.

"He was. He's too scared or too stupid to realise he needs to talk. I can't work out which."

"Let's follow him and see what he's up to."

Angus nodded. "Did you bring your computer?"

"I have my mini-computer. You want me to do the usual?"

"Yes."

They got back into Angus's car and followed Tom's car out of the car park. At the junction with the main road he sped away, swerved into the right-hand lane, overtaking a slow-moving family estate, and only stopped when the traffic lights ahead turned red. Angus pulled up behind him and the moment the lights changed, Tom shot off, driving at well over the speed limit. At the next roundabout he turned right, heading towards Matford, and disappeared into the distance. Angus wanted to keep up, but was unwilling to exceed the speed limit by more than a few miles per hour.

"Let's go to his home address," said Charlotte. "I'll try and hack his Wi-Fi."

Angus glanced at her. "Good idea. Although if he's going to work, we could go there."

"I'll call Trevor and get the addresses," Charlotte said.

She rang Trevor, and after a brief conversation, ended the call. "Guess where Tom works," she said. "The Comm Fab building."

Angus rolled his eyes.

A few minutes later, Charlotte and Angus approached the Comm Fab building. Outside it was Tom's car.

"Shall we go in?" Charlotte asked. "He clearly doesn't want to talk to us."

Angus didn't slow down but cruised past the building. "Let's go and hack his home W-Fi."

Charlotte grinned. "If you're encouraging me to hack, he's really got under your skin."

Angus didn't reply but followed Charlotte's directions to Tom's flat. It was at the quayside, in a large modern block. They parked in a nearby car park while Charlotte worked out which was Tom's Wi-Fi. "There are a few possibles. I need to get closer to the building to work out which is right. Inside the building would be even better."

"I'll take the car closer. Best you don't go inside: a building like this is bound to have CCTV. You don't want to be caught on camera."

"OK," Charlotte said. Angus pulled up on double yellow lines, as close to the building as possible.

It took Charlotte a few minutes to identify the right Wi-Fi, and then she set her hacking program to work. A few minutes later, "I'm in." She looked up from her computer and smiled at Angus. "Easier than James's. Let me have a sniff around, then I'll leave my spyware on his network."

Fifteen minutes later, she closed her computer. All done. There's nothing on his network at the moment, but when he connects, it will alert me."

Angus nodded.

"Shall we go home?" Charlotte asked.

"Not yet. I want to try James Finley. He's the only one we haven't spoken to, and he's behind the trolling messages to the club."

"Daniel, the IT guy, hasn't been in touch to say whether there have been any more messages."

"Phone him and find out."

Charlotte searched for his number and called him. "Daniel, it's Charlotte Lockwood. I'm looking into the abusive messages to the club. I wondered if there had been any more since I visited? Yes ... uh-huh ... OK.." She listened for a while. "OK, thanks. Bye." She ended the call and turned to Angus. "Yep, there have been loads and they're just as bad. They all saying that match-fixing is going on and the club ought to be ashamed."

"In that case," said Angus, "we'll definitely give James Finley another try."

Chapter Fifteen

Angus straightened his tie and knocked on James's door. Half a minute or so later, James answered it. "Yes?" He glanced at Angus, then his eyes fell on Charlotte.

"Don't I know you?" he asked. "You're from the council, aren't you?"

"Mr Finley, I'm Angus Darrow and this is my colleague Charlotte Lockwood. We're private investigators. We'd like to speak to you about the awards evening at the rugby club yesterday, and in particular about the death of Coach Clarke."

James stared at them for a moment. It was almost possible to see the cogs turning in his brain.

"Private investigators? Are you working with the police?"

"We're working for Devon Rugby, and we've been asked to speak to some of the people who were at the awards evening. I know you were there; I saw you."

"I don't see what it's got to do with me."

"You were there." Angus stated again.

His eyes narrowed. "I was. But I don't know who this coach was, and I didn't see anything."

"He visited you with Oliver Miller, Thomas Hunter and a man called Screwball a few days ago, so you do know him. Can we come in?"

James shook his head. "I don't think so. You're barking up the wrong tree." He looked round Charlotte and Angus, as though looking for someone, then closed the door on them.

Angus didn't move. "He's scared."

"Definitely."

"Shall we go home?"

"Yep. Let's get back."

"I'll drop you off, then I'm meeting Simon."

"Lucky you!" said Charlotte, with a grimace.

They walked back to the car and got in. Angus was about to start the engine when his phone beeped. He looked at the screen. A text, from a blocked number.

Screwball is called Gavin Brooks and lives in Wonford.

He held it up for Charlotte to read.

"Do you think it's true?"

Angus shrugged, and sent a text back. *Whoever you are, we need to talk.*

A minute later, another text arrived: *Not poss.*

"Well that was short and to the point," said Charlotte. "Interesting that they put a full stop, though. Good punctuation is important, even when sending secret texts."

"They're clearly scared." Angus put the phone in the side bucket of the door.

Charlotte nodded. "When you drop me off, I'll look into it."

. . .

When Angus had dropped Charlotte off he messaged Simon, who told him to come to the main police station in Exeter.

The building had been opened a few months before. Although Angus didn't miss the job, he was interested in having a look around the new building.

Simon took Angus through the station to his new office on the second floor. The building was immaculate. A lot of money had clearly been spent on it, all from the sale of the land surrounding the old building, which would be developed into houses.

They had passed through a communal space on the way to Simon's office, and as Angus sat down he realised that while he'd seen numerous detectives, he hadn't recognised any of them. Recruitment must have been working hard.

"How's things since last night?" Angus asked.

"Busy. I didn't get any sleep, and I'm running on caffeine at the moment."

"I remember the days," said Angus. "You want to know what I've been looking into at the rugby club?"

"I do. Didn't you say it was about abusive messages accusing the club of match-fixing?"

"That's right. We've managed to identify the person behind the messages, but so far we don't know why he's doing it. It's convoluted."

"Do you think there's a connection to the murder last night?" asked Simon.

"I don't know. However, a few days ago Coach Clarke and a couple of other players visited a house we were watching. The person behind the threats lives there: James Finley."

Simon stared at Angus. "How do you know this person was behind the threats?"

Angus opened his mouth, then froze. He couldn't betray Charlotte. "I can't tell you that," he said. "Rest assured, though, he is the culprit."

Simon picked up a pen and rolled it between his fingers. "Well, your partner is a cybersecurity expert, so I'm guessing she worked it out. I won't ask how. Anything else I should know?"

"Another local man called Screwball visited the house with the players and Coach Carter. We've just had a tip-off that his name is Gavin Brooks and he lives in Wonford. I overheard him pushing his way into the party and he wasn't welcome. We'll look into him, but we're pretty sure he wasn't there to help them with personal development."

"I'll add him to the list of people to look into. We're still waiting for the full autopsy results, but it was definitely murder."

"How long did the drug take to work?"

"About ten minutes, at most. It's likely he went to the toilet to take the drug and never came out. He might have been in the bathroom for a while. His wife can't remember how long he'd been gone before she noticed. She'd had a lot to drink."

"Has anyone admitted to selling him the drug?"

Simon laughed, without humour. "No. And there are no other prints on the canister. The strange thing is that we found a few other canisters in the car park, but none of them were chloroethane. They were all nitrous oxide."

"It does look like he was the target," said Angus. "It would be easy enough to spike a canister if he regularly bought recreational drugs. Who from, though?"

"I have to say that when you left the police, I thought I'd seen the last of you," Simon smiled. "We're working together almost as much as we did before."

Angus stood up. "Occupational hazard. If I find out anything else, I'll let you know."

"Thanks." Simon stood up too. "I'll see you out."

Charlotte had spent the afternoon looking into Screwball, or rather, Gavin Brooks. She'd gone the extra mile by producing a document on him as well as updating the conspiracy board.

When Angus got back from visiting Simon, she couldn't help herself. "How was Inspector Clouseau?" she asked.

Angus ignored her reference to the hapless policeman from the Pink Panther films. "He was fine, and it was definitely a highly toxic concentration of chloroethane that killed Coach Clarke."

"Nasty. I take it you gave him our update."

"Of course. I always co-operate with the police."

"So do I," Charlotte replied. "Even if they like to accuse innocent people of crimes they didn't commit."

Angus walked to the window and looked out. "You need to let it drop, you know, Charlotte. Resentment will only hurt you. Can't you speak to Misty about it? Get it all off your chest, then start afresh."

"I haven't spoken to Misty for a few weeks." Charlotte mused. There was a lot to update her therapist about.

Angus turned. "Did you find anything out about Gavin Brooks?"

Charlotte clapped her hands together. "Oh yes, here you are."

She handed him two sheets of A4 paper stapled together. On the front was a photo of Screwball. "Whoever texted you Screwball's real name was telling the truth. Meet Gavin Brooks, aka 'Screwball'. Aged twenty-nine, born and raised in Plymouth, he moved to Exeter four years ago. The advanced search on his background shows he's been in trouble with the police multiple times, starting when he was arrested for shoplifting aged fifteen. He progressed to possession of class C drugs, more petty theft, and handling stolen goods. But for the last three years, nothing."

Angus turned the page of the document Charlotte had handed him. "Any reason why he moved from Plymouth to Exeter?"

"Yes, actually, there is. He's listed on Companies House as part-director and owner of a gym in Exeter, a new branch of a company called 'Gym Palace'. It originally started in Plymouth and is expanding into South Devon and Exeter."

"Gym Palace?" Angus repeated.

"Yes. Looking at the website, it is rather plush, in a male ego-stroking sort of way."

Charlotte turned her screen round for Angus to see. The gym was kitted out with cardio machines, treadmills, ellipticals, stairclimbers and stationary bikes. More photos showed floor-to-ceiling mirrors with racks of free weights. The walls without mirrors were painted black and the lighting had a green tinge, giving the place a nightclub feel.

"He's involved in dodgy stuff." Charlotte said.

"How do you know?" Angus put the document on her desk.

"I can just tell. He's shifty."

"Well, we know that because of the meeting at James's house and perhaps because of what Oliver and Tom were talking about on the night of the party. But is there any other evidence apart from his childhood misdemeanours?"

Charlotte shook her head. "No."

"In that case, we'll start watching him and take it from there. I assume you'll want to hack his home and the gym?"

"Obviously. But I'll also send Grigore to join the gym under a false name, and report back. He's more likely to get info from there than Comm Fab. I'll ask him."

They were interrupted by Angus's phone ringing. The call was from a withheld number, and he answered it hoping it would be- whoever had texted him Screwball's real name.

"Mr Darrow? This is Exeter Council. We have some further information for you regarding the World War 2 bomb. The bomb disposal team have told us that the explosion will take place in two days' time at 1pm. Afterwards, building inspectors will check the nearby houses and you'll be allowed back into your home the day after."

Angus rubbed his forehead. That meant he'd be staying at Charlotte's for at least another three days. He reminded himself that there was no point in stressing over anything outside his control. "Thank you for letting me know," he said, and ended the call.

He turned to Charlotte. "Looks like you're stuck with me for at least three more days until the bomb is exploded, I'm afraid."

Charlotte smiled. "That's going to make a very loud bang."

Angus stood up. "I'll make dinner."

He cooked them both risotto. They used the breakfast bar in the kitchen for a change. As Charlotte sat down, Angus put a plate of the food in front of her.

"It smells divine," she said. "What's in it?"

Angus sat down next to her. "Well, rice."

"I gathered that. And...?"

"Cheese and roasted butternut squash."

Charlotte picked up her fork and tried it. "It tastes as good as it smells."

"It's just using some of the ingredients from my fridge." They sat in companionable silence for a few minutes, eating, until the sound of the front door opening and closing interrupted them.

Helena came into the kitchen and stopped when she saw Angus and Charlotte. "Hello," she said brightly. "Sorry for interruption. I go soon. Just come to collect food for refuge."

Angus stood up, "There's enough for you too if you'd like some. Why don't you join us?"

Helena looked over to Charlotte. "No, no. I have Pilates class later, I eat after that."

Charlotte nodded.

"See you tomorrow," Helena said and headed for the door with the food she'd come to collect.

"I just need to ask Helena something," Charlotte told Angus, and followed Helena outside.

"Zo, iz he still sleeping in spare room or your room?" Helena asked.

Charlotte grimaced. "His room, of course. As usual, he's the perfect gentleman, annoying as it is."

"Maybe he has a bad boy in there zomwhere."

Charlotte folded her arms. "He might be the one man who hasn't."

"Get him drunk. Zat work."

"I'm not getting him drunk! Anyway, he never has more than one drink. He's far too self-controlled."

Helena shrugged. "I have run out ideas, but he's in your house. Don't waste it." And she walked to her car.

Back inside, Charlotte finished her meal pondering Helena's words. There was no way she'd make a move on Angus. She'd done that once, and sworn never to do it again. Well, she'd kissed him at the party, but that was to cover for the eavesdropping. It didn't count. She felt butterflies in her stomach thinking about that kiss though. It might have been fleeting, but it had been glorious and she couldn't suppress the feeling of glee each time she remembered it. She'd caught him completely off-guard, but once he'd realised what she was doing, he'd kissed her back. He'd held her tighter too. It had been a glimpse into what might be. It hadn't felt like pretence, but she couldn't be sure.

They were friends and colleagues. Despite how she felt about him, Angus would have to make the first move. And he'd never indicated he felt anything more than friendship. Annoying as it was, Charlotte didn't want what they had to be ruined. She didn't know what she would do if she couldn't work with Angus any more. She'd gone from being a total mess to, well, almost sane.

Angus made her want to be a better person, and his steady, calm influence had made her see the lack of direction in her life since she'd sold the cybersecurity company and her marriage had fallen apart. And yet... Even on an exotic holiday to recover from being kidnapped, she'd missed him.

She'd just have to make sure that while Angus stayed in her house, he enjoyed his time with her. Maybe they could watch films together.

The next morning, Charlotte and Angus planned their next move: surveillance of Gavin 'Screwball' Brooks's home and hacking his Wi-Fi.

"I can get Grigore to take me," she said. "I don't need you to come."

"I want to have a look at the place," Angus said, just before biting into a piece of toast and Marmite.

Charlotte shrugged. "OK."

Grigore came into the house and headed for the coffee machine. "Hello, sweetie," said Charlotte. "How did joining the gym go last night?"

Grigore pressed the Latte button and the machine started to gurgle. "I join. I go this morning for induction."

Charlotte grimaced. "It so annoying when you join a gym and they make you have an induction even though you know how everything works."

Grigore put a mug under the coffee machine's spout and hot latte started to pour into the cup.

"When do you think it will be quietest to have a snoop around the office?" she asked him.

Grigore waited for the machine to stop and took a sip of his coffee. "It busy, but it open 24 hours and only staffed until 10pm. I let you in when they gone."

Charlotte clapped her hands. "Excellent."

Angus sighed. "Breaking and entering is illegal, you know, and they'll have CCTV everywhere."

She turned to him. "I'm not breaking and entering. I'm going to accidentally take out the cameras by cutting the internet connection, then deleting any evidence that I was there."

Angus folded his arms. "I don't like it, Charlotte. These are probably hardened criminals. If they find out what you did and who you are, they'll hurt you. We'll just watch them for now."

Charlotte frowned. "I'll be very careful and I won't get caught. Anyway, I might not have to break into the office. If I can get into their computer, I'll be able to see what they're up to without that."

"Charlotte, I can't tell you what to do, but we work together and I take the lead on all the investigations. That means you work for me. I don't want you breaking into this gym office. It's too dangerous."

Charlotte stared at him. "Why are you so cautious all of a sudden? Like I said, I probably won't need to break in anyway."

Grigore sat down on one of the breakfast-bar chairs. "Zey have office at back: they took me in to sign me up. They have one computer, one printer, and CCTV."

"See," Angus said in a 'told you so' tone.

Charlotte ignored him. "Anything else?"

"No."

"I'll go there after I've tried to hack Screwball's house, and get into the Wi-Fi," said Charlotte. "The gym does have Wi-Fi, doesn't it?"

"Yez, password on board as you go in."

"Excellent."

Angus drove them to Wonford. Gavin Brooks's address was a flat in the eastern part. The building was a 1960s monstrosity, its only redeeming feature that they'd only built one. They sat outside the block of flats and watched the entrance. "Which one do you think is his?" Charlotte asked.

"We need to go in and look," said Angus. "But first, we watch."

Charlotte looked at the main door. "How long do we watch for?" she asked, ten seconds later.

"Long enough to get a feel for the place."

Charlotte craned her neck and inspected it, "Well, I'm guessing from the area and the way it looks that the people living here are not well off."

The main door opened and a young woman in active wear and a puffer jacket wheeled out a pram.

"There must be about fifty flats," said Angus. It'll be almost impossible to work out if anyone is visiting Screwball." He sighed.

"The only option is to hack his Wi-Fi," said Charlotte.

"If he has any."

"Let's go in and see. I can work out if he has one from outside his door."

Angus nodded. "We'll wear fluorescent bibs. If anyone asks what we're doing, we can pretend we're surveyors."

They got out of the car, put on hi-vis jackets and went inside.

They followed the signs to find Gavin Brooks's flat. The building was cold and unwelcoming, and as they climbed the stairs their steps echoed around them.

Screwball's flat was on the third floor, the first door in a row of five. Angus put his arm out to stop Charlotte walking in front of it, then pointed to the spy hole in the door.

Charlotte took out her tablet computer and tapped at the screen. She looked up to find Angus watching her. "I'm not getting anything here. I need to walk along the hall to double check."

Angus nodded and she walked past him to the furthest door. She tapped the screen again, then slowly walked back to Angus. "Nothing," she whispered. "He must be using a mobile phone for internet access."

"All right, let's go," said Angus.

Just as they started to walk down the stairs, they heard Screwball's front door open.

"Quick," Angus grabbed Charlotte's hand and hurried her down. They'd made it down one flight before they heard voices above them and the door close. It wasn't until they were out of the building and heading to Angus's car when they looked back to see who had been behind them. It was a man in his twenties, hands in the front pocket of his hoody. It wasn't anyone they knew.

"Shit, that was a bit scary." Charlotte felt her hands shake and her heart thumping.

Angus clicked his key fob and the car doors opened. "We need to be more careful. We were lucky it wasn't him. Let's go to Gym Palace in Matford."

It was located on a quiet side street. There was a small carpark in front, and it shared a building with a tyre fitter's.

Angus drove past and turned the car round, then parked on the road outside so that they could see the gym building and its main doors.

"We need to watch the place for a short time and decide how we'll get inside and look around," said Angus. "There'll be so many members of the public going in and out that it's better to get inside. *If* we go inside."

Charlotte was already tapping the screen of her computer. "When was the last time you used a gym?" she asked.

"I can't remember," Angus replied. "I hate them. I'd rather do any other exercise than go to a gym."

"You've never used a treadmill to run?"

"Once or twice, but I hated it."

Charlotte nodded slowly. "I quite like gyms, but when I went, you couldn't get near the free weights for all the men. Some did ladies-only hours, but they were always at awkward times. Mind you, I used to work such long hours that all the hours were awkward."

Angus leaned over. "Well, now you could buy your own gym and make it 100% female."

She stared at him, her eyes widening. "That's a *brilliant* idea. Oh my God, why didn't I think of that?" She stared into the distance, thinking. "It wouldn't cost that much to set one up. All the staff would be female, too, and I'll pay better than most."

Angus rolled his eyes. "Of course you will."

Charlotte's computer pinged and she looked down. "They have Wi-Fi and Grigore told me the password. It won't be hard to access the main computer."

"Not for you."

"Bingo! I'm in. Oh, that was so easy." She flexed her fingers. "OK, I'm going to snoop around." She tapped the screen a few times. "Hmm, nothing much so far..."

Angus looked at her screen, but all he could see was text.

"There's not much here. Software they use for the members, MS Office, email. Not much else. That's disappointing."

"It's not likely they'd keep a record of their criminal activity on the computer."

Charlotte grimaced. "You're right. We could put a bug in the office and listen in to what they're saying."

"A bug?"

"Yep." She pulled her handbag onto her lap. "I have one or two here, just in case."

Angus stared at her in amazement. "You seriously want to put a bug in their office."

"Yes." Charlotte smiled. "Why not?"

"It's illegal."

Charlotte snorted. "These are criminals. What are they going to do if they find out? Tell the police?"

Angus sighed and rubbed his forehead. "They'll find out who you are and deal with you as they see fit, without police involvement. Anyway, how do you propose to get the bug into the office? Don't say Grigore. He deserves better than to be tasked with something like that."

"Hmm." Charlotte considered. "I could go in and sign up. Grigore said they took him into the office when he joined. You distract them, and I'll plant it somewhere."

"No. Besides, how will it transmit what it's picking up?"

Charlotte grinned. "I thought you weren't interested in the technical details. I could tell you, but your eyes would glaze over."

Angus started the car. "We'll go home and start proper surveillance in another way."

"We'll need help for that," Charlotte replied. "Do you know anyone?"

Angus pulled away from the kerb. "Not at the moment. But that's what we'll do."

Chapter Sixteen

When they got home, Angus went to his room and Charlotte to hers. She was annoyed at him for whisking her off before she could plant a bug in the gym, but she wasn't giving up.

She thought about getting Grigore to drive her back then remembered he was known there. It wouldn't do for him to be seen dropping her off. Instead, she would drive herself in the Volvo.

An hour later, she walked into Gym Palace and stood by the welcome desk.

A member of staff came over. "Can I help?" He was short but stocky, with neatly barbered hair, wearing a tight T-shirt with the Gym Palace logo. His name badge said *Ryan*, and he looked about twenty.

"Hello, Ryan," she said brightly. "I'm interested in joining the gym." Inside the gym were half a dozen people, all men, working out. Most were in the free-weights area, watching themselves in the mirror as they lifted dumbbells or bars. One man was on a weights machine, lifting with his legs, his face screwing up with effort every time he moved. Music blared from the six screens attached to the walls, showing a music video from a singer she'd never heard of.

"Sure," said Ryan. "Would you like to have a look around?"

"Absolutely." Charlotte linked arms with him. "You know, you remind me of my son: young, intelligent, and very fit. My eldest plays football for his university. Which team do you support?"

Ryan let himself be led towards the weights area. "Er, Plymouth Argyle."

Charlotte winked at him. "Your secret's safe with me. Don't tell anyone around here, though! Ooh, I love the dark walls. They give the place a great feel, a bit like a nightclub. Not that I go to those any more – far too old now."

Ryan gave her a half smile. "Have you been a gym member before?"

Charlotte let go of his arm. "More times than I care to remember. A woman like me, in middle age, needs to look after herself as much as a younger woman. I do it for my darling husband: he loves me in short dresses."

Ryan scuttled forward. "This is the weights area," he said. "They're the latest dumbbells: laser cut."

To Charlotte, they looked like any other dumbbells. "Laser-cut dumbbells! Excellent! I'll sign up."

"Er, don't you want to see the rest of the place?"

"No, I'm good. I like the place – or rather, the palace," she said, with a giggle. She grabbed Ryan's arm and led him to the office before he could say no.

The office was small, with little else but the computer Charlotte had hacked into earlier. She sat down in the swivel chair in front of it. "If you give me the membership form, I'll fill it in. Then I can come ASAP."

Ryan opened a desk drawer, took out a membership form and pen and handed them to Charlotte.

Charlotte looked up and down the form. "Just give me a few minutes and I'll have this all done." Ryan sat on the other chair, by the wall.

Charlotte looked at him. "Would you mind leaving me alone while I do this? It's just that I have dyspraxia and I have terrible handwriting. I need time to concentrate so that you can read what I've put."

Ryan nodded. "Yeah sure. I understand, I'm dyslexic myself." He got up. "Give me a shout when you're done."

Charlotte waited a few seconds after he'd gone before looking for a home for the bug. Under or behind the table was too obvious. She looked up. The ceiling light was round, with a ridge. That would be perfect, but she'd have to stand on a chair to reach it. She took the bug out of her pocket. It was the size of her little fingernail, black, with a tiny antenna that would transmit to their computer then over the internet to her secret server in Russia. If anyone found it, they'd never trace it back to her. She took out a small piece of sticky tac, stuck it to the bug, then moved Ryan's chair and stood on it.

She easily reached the lamp and stuck the bug on the flat part of the light. It was invisible from below.

She stepped down, her heart pounding, and left the office. Ryan was talking to one of the men in the weights area.

Charlotte waved her phone as she strode past. "So sorry – just had a phone call from my elderly mother. She needs me to sort something out. I'll come back and finish the form!"

She hurried to her car, got in, and breathed a sigh of relief. The whole thing had taken about ten minutes. She retrieved her computer from the glove box and clicked a few buttons to check the bug was working. It was.

When Charlotte got home, she went straight to the kitchen and made herself a cup of coffee. There was no sign of Angus. If he asked where she'd been, she'd make up an excuse. She didn't want to lie to him, but if she found out something important, he'd be upset.

She went to her computer and checked the feed from the bug. She'd set it up so that it would record speech, turn it into text and log it on a feed. So far, the only words spoken in the room had been "Yeah, OK."

About an hour later, Angus came into the study. "You OK to talk for a moment?" He asked.

Charlotte was at the window, looking out. "Sure."

"We need to start proper surveillance of Screwball."

Charlotte frowned. "We agreed that already, didn't we?"

"I'll contact some old colleagues to see if they're interested in helping."

"I can ask Grigore and Helena to help," she said.

Angus stood silent for a moment. "I know," he said, eventually, and put his hands in his trouser pockets. "Look, I know we could ask them, but don't you think we should give them a break? We shouldn't expect them to help us every time."

"What do you mean?" Charlotte's frown deepened. "They like helping."

Angus walked over to her. "They usually do anything you ask. But maybe they don't want to sit for hours in a car, watching for Screwball."

"They won't mind, really they won't."

Angus raised his eyebrows. "Are you sure?"

"What are you trying to say?"

Angus shrugged. "They think the world of you, but maybe for once you shouldn't ask them. Maybe they just don't want to upset you."

"They both know they can say no to me. " Charlotte shifted from foot to foot. "Are you accusing me of taking advantage because ... because I've got money?" She felt anger rising in her, making her frame tense and rigid.

Angus folded his arms. "I suppose I am." He came closer. "Look, I know you're all tight with each other and I like them both, but I don't want to take advantage of them. It's one thing for you to help me, but they weren't supposed to be part of the deal."

Charlotte gaped at him. "I don't take advantage of them!" She looked out of the window, then back at him. "Do I?"

"I know Grigore is your driver and he'll take you wherever you want, but we've been relying on them both too much recently. If we need more help, I should get someone else on board."

Charlotte frowned: she didn't like that idea. It was much better with just the two of them. "Who are you thinking of?"

"Like I said: an ex-colleague who can do some of the legwork."

She shrugged. "Well, it's your company. You can hire whoever you like."

Angus gave her a reassuring smile.

"Do you have anyone in mind?" she asked.

"A few people. I'll give a few of them a call now." He left the room.

Charlotte walked back to her desk and sat down. She

gazed at the screen, but saw nothing. Their conversation circled in her head. Had she been taking advantage of Helena and Grigore? She didn't think so. They both seemed happy enough, and in fact Helena had volunteered to help at the rugby club awards night.

Charlotte checked the bug from Gym Palace again. The conversations it had picked up were pretty monotonous: rota scheduling, office banter, and a new member signing up. Nothing out of the ordinary. Perhaps the bug had been a waste of time. If Screwball was up to no good, he didn't seem to get up to anything at the gym. Maybe Angus was right, and he needed longer-term surveillance.

She watched new text scroll up the screen.

We've got about ten minutes.

That's not long enough.

It is for me. Haha.

Someone might come in.

They won't.

Oooo I like that, don't stop.

Oh God, they weren't, were they?

Ooh, yes that feels so good.

The last thing she needed was to hear, or rather read, people having sex via the bug. She minimised the screen. She'd come back later, when hopefully it would be over.

Charlotte went for a walk round the garden to get some

fresh air and sit in the sun before it set, then returned to the computer half an hour later.

Thankfully, whatever had happened earlier was indeed over. She read through the transcript of the last twenty minutes.

What time is kick-off on Saturday?

4pm. I've got tickets for us all in the executive box. And I'll be watching Oliver and Tom to make sure they what we told them.

Yeah, well, they'd better do it. They know the consequences if they don't.

What if they don't, though? I mean, there's too much to lose. Mr Ling will kill us.

Mr Ling thinks he's the kingpin, but he ain't. He just thinks he is. I'm going to make him so much money, he'll adopt me.

Laughter

Seriously though, we need to up the pressure on them.

What are you suggesting?

They know we'll hurt them if they don't do what we ask in the match, but there's a sure fire way to make sure they do exactly what we want.

What?

Use their family as leverage.

What you thinking then?

Look, we only hurt family if we have to. That's always been our way. The innocent only get hurt as a last resort, we know that. Luckily we've only had to use this tactic a few times in the past. But what matters is we can use them as security to make sure we get what we want.

. . .

Charlotte reread the text, then listened to the audio recording. Yes, that really was what they'd said. She wasn't sure one of them was Screwball, but Angus would know. He'd heard him talking at the party.

She had to tell Angus. It was the only way. She'd kept the bug from him and she felt a bit bad about that, but he'd be pleased when he saw the result.

She went upstairs. "Knock knock," she said, at Angus's open door.

Angus was stretched out on the bed, his pen and notebook in his hands. He put them down and looked at her.

"There's something you need to see, or rather hear," said Charlotte tentatively. "It's to do with the case."

Angus swung his legs to the floor. "Sure."

He followed her down to the study and watched her as she took a seat.

"Sit down," she said. Her throat felt tight. "Ok, you know you said we shouldn't put a bug in Gym Palace? Well ...I put a bug in Gym Palace."

Angus regarded her. "You're joking right?"

Charlotte took a deep breath. "No."

He stood up and walked to the window, his hand on his forehead. "I told you not to plant a bug."

"I know, but why does it matter now? What matters is that it's picked up vital information for the case, and they're about to do something *really* bad."

Angus regarded her, his face angry. "When did you do it?"

Charlotte paused for a moment then answered. "I sneaked out about an hour after we got back."

"So not only did you you purposefully do exactly what I asked you not to do, you did it almost straight away."

"Only because I knew we'd get some vital info - "

"When are you going to stop doing everything that's illegal? It's getting ridiculous. One day, you are going to get caught, and we'll both end up in prison. Have you any idea what prison is like for former police officers?"

Realisation of why he was reacting like this dawned on her, "Is that what you're worried about? I've told you, I won't get caught and I'd never admit you knew what I was doing."

"That is so arrogant and that is exactly what is going to get you caught one day."

"I've told you, I know what I'm doing. I know how to hide everything I do."

"How exactly?"

"It's technical. You wouldn't understand and you'd tell me to stop explaining, you always do."

"So this is my fault now for being a technophobe?"

"No, I'm just saying that I know what I'm doing and you have to trust me."

He turned around and stared out the window. The moment she'd planted the bug, she'd known it was wrong, but she also knew it would get the info they needed. And anyway, they were clearly a nasty gang who were up to lots of criminal activity and possibly even murder.

After a long pause, he turned around sat in the chair opposite her then leaned forward and took hold of both her hands.

"If we're going to continue working together, you need to do what I ask. This isn't a partnership, and you don't have equal say. You still work for me, and I lead the investigations."

Charlotte opened her mouth to speak, but he put a hand up to stop her. "It doesn't matter if you don't get caught, what matters is it's illegal. I do things by the book, and it might take longer and be frustrating for you, but that's just the way I work."

She frowned, "So can I still hack Wi-Fis?"

He dropped his head for a moment then lifted it, meeting her eye. "No. But most importantly you can't use bugs. You have to promise me you won't use them again. I mean it."

Charlotte considered. She'd never used them before anyway. But not hacking Wi-Fis. It was her signature hack, mainly because it was so easy.

But the thought of not working with Angus, not having him around in her life was far worse.

"Alright. I promise." She found herself saying. He let go of her hands and sat back.

"So what about the info I found out from the bug? I mean, it's pretty important. And seeing as I've got it before I promised not to use bugs, we can't ignore it."

Angus looked to the computer then back at Charlotte. "Show me what you have first."

"Read this." She turned the screen around.

Angus's brow furrowed as he read. "This reads as if two people are about to have sex."

"What?" Charlotte turned the screen back. "Oh, sorry, it's the bit after that."

Charlotte clicked the mouse, then turned the screen round again and Angus read.

When he'd finished, she played the audio. "Is it Screwball?"

"It does sound like him, but I can't be completely sure. I only heard him speak for a short time at the party that night. There was a lot of background noise too."

"Don't you think it sounds like they're making the players do something during the match?" she asked.

Angus nodded. "It does. It also sounds like they are threatening their family too." He looked at his watch. "We could speak to the players. Is there a match tonight? It's mid-week."

"Yes, they've got a late match. They won't say anything. It sounds as if Screwball has some sort of hold over them."

"We could try James Finley again."

"Do you think he'll talk?" Charlotte asked.

Angus stood up. "Last time I tried, he slammed the door in my face. This time, we have to make him."

Chapter Seventeen

"Why don't you let me try this time?" Charlotte said, on the doorstep of James Finley's house. "He might not slam the door on a woman."

Angus considered, then motioned her forward.

She knocked three times. When the door opened, James looked at her and relief washed over his face.

"Hello, remember me? Charlotte Lockwood, private investigator. Can I come in?"

James stared at her for a moment. "Look, I already told you that I don't know anything about Coach Clarke dying. I want you to go away. Stop coming here."

"Why? Are you worried that Screwball might see you talking to us?"

James's eyes widened. "I've no idea who that is."

"Yes you do. And I know you've been sending threatening messages to the rugby club about match -fixing."

"Shh." James looked into the street in the same way as the last time they'd called.

"Why don't you let us in?" Charlotte asked. "Then we can have a quiet conversation."

He paused, then ushered them through to the kitchen-diner.

His house was smartly decorated. The hallway had a dark laminate floor, the kitchen, pristine white units. The radio was playing in the background and his laptop sat on the dining-room table.

"I told you last time that I had nothing to do with that man's death," James said. "Why don't you just leave me alone?"

"Look, James, we don't know whether you had anything to do with Coach Clarke's death, but you're clearly very nervous that we're here," said Charlotte, softly. "Who were you looking for when you answered the door?"

He stepped back. "What? I wasn't looking for anyone."

"You were." Charlotte moved forward. "I can see you're scared," she said, in an even softer voice, and touched his arm.

James ran his hand through his hair.

"We know that you've been sending threatening messages to the rugby club about match-fixing. There must be a reason, and maybe we can help. Why don't you start by telling us about the Wednesday Night Club?"

He stared at her. "What? How do you know about that?"

"Because, as I said, we've been investigating your threatening messages."

James's mouth fell open. "What messages? I haven't sent any messages to the club." He folded his arms, feet planted firmly apart.

"You have, and we have proof," said Charlotte.

"Proof?"

"I'm afraid so. I hacked your VPN and it led me straight to you."

"You hacked a VPN?" James didn't look convinced.

Charlotte shrugged. "That's what happens when you use a dodgy provider from Russia."

James stared at Charlotte and she held his gaze. "There's no point denying it."

James let out a sigh.

"Why don't we sit down," said Angus. "Then you can tell us why you've been accusing the rugby club."

James nodded and they sat down at the dining-room table. James shut his laptop, then sat with his legs spread. "I suppose you're taking your evidence to the police," he said, his tone flat.

Angus took out his notebook and pen. "We need you to tell us all about the Wednesday Night Club, and why Screwball, Coach Clarke, Oliver Miller and Thomas Hunter were here a few days ago."

James raised his eyebrows. "Have you been watching my house?"

Charlotte and Angus exchanged glances.

"So you have been watching my house. Otherwise, how would you know they all came here a few days ago?"

"We're here to get information, that's all."

"Information you'll take to the police?" The volume of James's voice rose.

"We're not going to the police," said Angus. "We're working for the rugby club. We just want to know why you've been sending them threatening messages about match-fixing."

"Because they are!" James shouted. He leaned forward and put his elbows on the table. "I can't tell you anything else."

"Who's threatening you?" Angus asked.

James looked up at him. "I can't tell you."

"Is it Screwball?"

James's face said more than words.

"It's Screwball," Charlotte said. "Look, we know he isn't a nice man, and he has his fingers in all sorts of pies. Is he part of the Wednesday Night Club?"

James hesitated for a moment. "Yeah."

"What happens at the club?" asked Angus.

"We drink, play poker, watch films. Have a laugh, you know?"

"How did you get to be part of the club?" asked Charlotte. "It's normally just players and coaches, isn't it?"

James shrugged. "Yeah. Oliver started it a couple of years ago. It's exclusive: not all the players get asked and nobody else knows about it." His expression hardened. "I'm not saying anything else. If anyone catches you here, I'll be in big trouble."

"No-one will know we were here. Screwball isn't watching you," Angus said.

"How do you know?"

"So it's Screwball you're scared of," Angus said.

"I hate him," James muttered. "I wish I'd never met him."

"What hold does he have over you?" Charlotte asked softly.

James closed his eyes and sighed. "I can't say. He's not the sort of man you want to cross."

"We worked that out a while ago," said Angus. "Look, we're going round in circles. Why don't you start from the beginning? If you don't want to tell us what Screwball has on you, that's fine. But there's more going on here and we know you're involved."

James looked up sharply. "I haven't broken any laws."

"Go ahead, then," said Angus.

"I knew Tom from school, although I was a few years above him. We've been pals since he was eleven and I was thirteen and we stayed in touch. About a year ago he mentioned that every Wednesday night he and some of the other rugby players met up to drink and do stuff. Fun stuff. I was going through a bad patch at the time: I'd split up with my girlfriend. So he invited me to try and cheer me up. Going there was the biggest mistake of my life."

He paused. Charlotte and Angus waited for him to gather his thoughts, and eventually he spoke again. "At first, it was all great. We'd have a drinking session, hang out, and play pool. Sometimes we'd play poker. Just a bit of fun. No actual money was involved; it was more about the kudos of winning. But then it got more serious. Instead of casino chips, we started to put real money in. That was when Screwball started coming."

"So the poker stakes got higher when he came along?" Angus asked.

"Yeah. The whole atmosphere changed when he turned up."

"Who invited him to join the group?"

"He never said, but I'm sure it was Tom."

"Do you think he was pressured into asking him?"

James shrugged. "Maybe. I dunno. I thought maybe Screwball was in the same position as me: needing time out in the week with friends."

"So the stakes got higher and real money was used. What happened next?" Angus asked.

James's expression darkened. "Screwball kept winning. Every single game."

Angus tapped his pen on the notebook. "Did he suddenly start winning, or was he always good at it?"

"He's a two-bit nobody who thinks he's someone," James said, a sneer on his face. "He thinks he can push people around. And I think he was cheating."

"How much did he win from you?" Charlotte asked.

"A lot. Enough to make me do his bidding. He doesn't need it, though. He's involved in all sorts of things."

"Drugs?" Angus asked.

"I wouldn't be surprised. He's that sort of lowlife. Most of his money comes from illegal lending." James's gaze fell. "I didn't tell you that."

"How do you know?"

James looked at them both."Are you taking this to the police?"

"Everything you tell us here is in the strictest confidence," said Angus. "We don't work for the police. We're just trying to find out why you threatened to tell everyone about match-fixing, and work out whether that has anything to do with Coach Clarke being murdered."

"I didn't kill Lee. I would never... How was he killed?"

Charlotte and Angus looked at each other. "The police haven't released that information yet," said Angus, "but they do think it's murder."

"Shit. I told him something would happen if he didn't keep his trap shut."

"Was he involved with the match-fixing?" asked Angus.

"Yeah, but he hated it. He owed Screwball money, but none of them have any choice. Screwball said he'd kill them if they blabbed. And he did."

"You think Screwball killed Lee Clarke?"

"Yeah. And I'm next, aren't I?" His voice cracked, then dissolved into sobs.

They let James cry for a while. Then Charlotte delved into her bag, pulled out a packet of tissues, and handed one to James.

"Thanks." He wiped his eyes.

"Is that why you were sending the messages?" She asked. "A cry for help?"

James nodded. "I didn't know what else to do. I thought that if the club knew there was match-fixing, they'd look into it. I didn't want to get anyone in trouble, but we were stuck in a corner. We all owe him money."

"Do you know if Coach Clarke took drugs at the Wednesday Night Club?"

"No-one did. Drugs were banned. The players couldn't let that sort of thing affect their fitness, and they get tested. It was just alcohol."

"So if Screwball was making the others fix matches, what did he make you do?"

James stared at Angus. "I'm an accountant."

"You're his accountant? I thought you were a Business Planning and Strategic Funding Consultant?"

"It's a fancy name for an accountant. I don't look after his legitimate business interests. Just his money lending. For now."

"How many people owe him money?"

"A few hundred in Exeter and double that in Plymouth. He has lots of business in both towns."

"What about the gyms?"

"They're used for money laundering."

Angus put his pen down and rubbed his forehead. "So he's controlling you, lending money illegally – no doubt charging extortionate interest – and he's coercing rugby players into match-fixing? Anything else?"

James shook his head, "Not that I know of."

"Does he sell drugs?"

"I don't know. I've never seen him do it, but I wouldn't put it past him." He fidgeted in his chair. "Can you go now? I've told you everything I know."

"I've got one more question." Angus tapped his pen on the notebook again. "We know that Screwball is threatening Oliver and Thomas to make them fix a match - probably tonight's game. Do you know what he's doing to make sure they comply? Is it just threatening them?"

James swallowed. "Not exactly. But I've heard him say that if they didn't do as he asked, he'd make sure they never played rugby again."

Charlotte winced. "But Thomas is huge! He's built like an American-style fridge-freezer."

"He wouldn't do it himself. He has muscle. He's made a mess of a few people who owe him money and don't pay up."

"How many men does he have to do his bidding?" Angus asked.

"Three or four that I know of." James grimaced. "They're nasty."

Angus closed his notebook and put it in his jacket pocket. "You need to stop sending messages to the club." Angus looked at James's closed laptop. "Leave it to us."

"If Screwball finds out I blabbed, he'll kill me too. Promise me you won't say anything."

"We promise," said Angus. "The last thing we want is for anyone else to get hurt."

James stood up and they followed him to the front door. "If he finds out you were here, I'm a dead man."

"Try not to worry," Angus said. "We're closing in on him. Promise me you won't do anything stupid."

James nodded, and closed the door behind them.

Chapter Eighteen

Angus and Charlotte went straight back to Angus's car and drove away.

Angus drove in silence until they were far enough from James's house not to be spotted if Screwball did come by. Then he pulled over at the side of the road. He sat silent, staring forwards.

He didn't turn to Charlotte until a full two minutes later. "I've got a bad feeling about this," he said. "My gut instinct is that he's threatening the players' families more than the players."

Charlotte shivered. "That's horrible."

"There's no way he could threaten them in the club. It's not his turf. So when you picked up their conversation, they could only have been talking about the wives or girlfriends."

"What do you mean?"

"I'm not sure. But I think we should check on Oliver and Tom's partners."

Charlotte nodded. "It won't hurt."

"Can you find Oliver and Tom's addresses? I can't remember them."

Charlotte took her tablet computer from her bag. "I'll look now. I have them in the background research." She tapped the screen and located them quickly.

Angus looked at his watch. "We'll try Tom's first. The kick-off is in a few minutes."

"Why are they playing on a weekday evening, anyway?" asked Charlotte.

"The original game a month ago was cancelled. This is the re-scheduled game."

Charlotte put the address into her satnav app and they arrived fifteen minutes later.

Chapter Nineteen

Angus parked outside the block of flats at the Quayside where they'd visited before.

"Shouldn't we call the police?" Charlotte asked.

"We have no evidence, except for the conversation from the gym – which we shouldn't know about – and lots of assumptions."

"Wouldn't your old sergeant believe you? You could tell him it's a hunch."

Angus considered this. "He probably would listen to me. We had a good working relationship and he knows I wouldn't waste his time."

"Call him, then."

"I will if I think there's a threat," said Angus. "Let's see if we can look inside the flat. And when I say we, I mean me."

Charlotte scrunched her mouth up. "Why not me, too?"

"I don't want to put us both at risk. Anyway, we don't even know they're here. Tom's girlfriend is probably at the match." He undid his seat belt. "Stay here – I mean it. But if I'm not back in five minutes, dial 999."

Angus got out of the car and approached the communal entrance. He tried it, but it was locked. At the side was a panel with buzzers for all the flats. He pressed a random one, then a moment later a voice came out of the speaker.

"Yeh?"

"Hi, Amazon delivery for your neighbour but they're not answering, can you let me in so I can leave the parcel?"

There was a moment of silence then, "Yeh."

The door clicked and Angus was in.

He made his way up a flight of stairs to Tom's flat and stood outside it for a moment. Then he knocked loudly.

Several knocks later the door opened. A burly man in his late forties wearing a tight black t-shirt and jeans, eyed Angus. "Yeah?"

"Hi, is Rachel in?"

The man frowned a little. "Why?"

"I'm her uncle. I was just passing and thought I'd drop in."

"She's busy."

"Could you ask her to come to the door just for a minute? I wanted to give her an early birthday present. She's my only niece."

The man leaned against the door frame. "You can give it to me."

Angus drew himself up. "And you are?"

"None of your business."

"I think it is." Angus tried to peer around him and failed. "Is Tom in, then?"

"No, he isn't."

"So what are you doing here?"

"Look, mate, just scarper. She's in and she's busy." He stepped back and slammed the door.

Angus deliberated what he should do next. He could try the door again, but the man who'd answered looked like he could do serious harm to whoever he liked. Or rather didn't like. He went back outside and walked towards the car. He stopped for a moment and glanced up to Tom's flat and saw a woman looking out of the window. Then a burly figure grabbed the woman by the shoulder and pulled her away.

Angus hurried back to the car and filled Charlotte in.

"You have to call Simon," she said.

"I know." Angus took out his phone. The call went straight to voicemail. "Simon, it's Angus. Call me as soon as you get this: it's urgent."

"Typical," said Charlotte. "Whenever you need the police, they're busy. How can we get her out of there?"

"We can't, and they might be holding Oliver's girlfriend too. We need to let the police deal with it. Meanwhile, we have to stop the match." He put his seat belt on and started the car.

Charlotte stared at him. "Where are your priorities?"

Angus looked across at her. "It's the only way the players won't throw the match. If they can't play, they can't lose. Therefore, they won't endanger their girlfriends."

"How will we going to stop a rugby match?" Charlotte put a hand to her head. "There's no way we can do it."

"I'll just have to convince Trevor," said Angus, and put his foot on the accelerator.

Chapter Twenty

It took longer than usual to get across Exeter. All the traffic lights were red, and the city was busy. When they reached the rugby club junction, they were stopped by a temporary barrier staffed by a security guard.

Angus pulled up and wound down his window. He heard the sound of the crowd in the stadium, the game had already started.

The guard bent to speak to him. "Are you here for the game, sir? Parking for the general public is in one of the temporary car parks. Follow the signs."

"We're not here for the game," said Angus. "We need to speak to Trevor Holland."

The guard smiled. "Mr Holland will be watching the game, sir."

Angus sighed. "I know: we work for him. Is Nigel working today?"

"Nigel? Yes, he is."

"Can you speak to him, please? He knows me. My name is Angus Darrow. Tell him I'm the private investigator from the night of the party. It's urgent and I need help."

The man stared at Angus for a moment, then felt for his radio. Wait a moment, sir." He stood up and walked a short distance away. Then he returned a minute later and bent to the window.

"Drive in and park in the reserved section. Nigel will meet you at the front entrance."

The barrier lifted and Angus parked near the entrance. Nigel was standing by the door. "You need help?"

"Can you take us to Trevor, please. I need to speak to him."

"This way." Nigel beckoned them inside and the sound of the crowd in the stadium disappeared.

Nigel led them up two flights of stairs, then down a corridor and into a large conference room labelled '*Executive Suite*.' He pointed to a huge glass window showing the stadium. On the glass door beside it, a sticker said '*Executive Box*'.

Angus opened the door and the noise of the crowd hit him. There was an amazing view of the pitch, and for a moment he was transfixed by the panorama of the players and the stadium. Then he remembered why he was there and looked for Trevor. The box had two rows of ten seats and he was in the middle of the front row, sandwiched between two men.

Angus stepped down, got the attention of the man beside Trevor, and gestured to convey what he wanted. The man nudged Trevor and pointed at Angus. Trevor sidled out of the seat, then followed Angus into the executive suite.

"What is it?" He snapped. "The game's underway."

"You need to stop the match," said Angus.

Trevor gave a sarcastic laugh.

"I'm serious."

Trevor snorted. "Don't be ridiculous. We can't abandon any game unless there's a serious incident."

Charlotte stepped forward. "What about match-fixing?"

"What? Look, I've already told you: there's no match-fixing going on."

"There is, and it's happening right now," she said. "Players are being pressured into it. Coach Clarke was killed because he tried to expose it."

"I don't believe you." Trevor walked towards the door, then turned. "Can you prove it?"

Angus remembered James Finley sobbing at his own dining-room table, and his assurance to James that he wouldn't say anything.

"I knew it," Trevor muttered. He opened the glass door that led out to the executive box. "By the way, you're both fired." His eyes gleamed, and he let the door close behind him.

"Stupid bastard," Charlotte said loudly.

Angus sighed. "Well, that didn't work. Got any other ideas?"

Charlotte pondered. "I could kill the lights." The sky was dark enough now for the stadium to need the floodlights.

Angus raised his eyebrows. "How? Will you hack into the network?"

"Don't need to," Charlotte said proudly. "I already have total access to their computer systems remember?"

Angus frowned. "What? How?"

Charlotte beamed at him. "My USB flash drive, with the worm virus... I have a back door to the entire stadium and can switch the flood lights off. No one can play if it's pitch black. No pun intended."

Angus stared at her for a moment. "Do it."

Charlotte took out her tablet computer, sat down at a nearby table, and started typing.

Angus glanced at her screen. It was all Greek to him.

"Dammit," said Charlotte. She looked out at the stadium. The lights were still on and the game was still in progress.

"What's wrong?"

"Hang on a minute." She typed, paused, and again. "I'm trying to find out where the lights are controlled. It's not easy. They haven't named things very well. But... Gotcha!"

Everything fell into darkness.

Silence fell over the entire stadium.

"Oops," said Charlotte, "I killed the emergency lighting too. I need to get that back up before someone hurts themselves."

A few seconds later, the emergency lighting came on, illuminating the exits, but the pitch was only barely lit. The floodlights were gone. Charlotte and Angus were still in the dark, except for the glow from her tablet computer and the emergency-exit sign.

Someone stumbled in from the executive box, and as they approached they realised it was Trevor. "What the hell is going on?" he shouted.

"You wouldn't stop the game, so I did it for you," said Charlotte.

"You stupid bitch! You can't just stop a rugby match!"

"I think you'll find I can."

Trevor lunged for Charlotte but Angus blocked his way. "Stay away from her," he said.

Trevor tried to get around him. "Put the floodlights back on now!" he shouted, raising his arms.

"What's going on, Trev?" said a voice from the door.

Screwball came out of the executive box, using a smartphone as a torch.

Trevor looked towards him. "She killed the floodlights," he said, pointing at Charlotte. "She's trying to stop the game."

Charlotte smiled. "I have stopped the game."

Screwball stepped forwards. "Look love, I dunno how you did it, but you need to put the lights back on."

"No!" Charlotte shouted back. "That match has been fixed and it can't go on. It *won't* go on."

Trevor tried to dodge Angus again. "Look, Oliver and Tom have nothing to worry about."

Angus stared at him. "How did you know it was Oliver and Tom?"

Trevor's brow furrowed. "Er, you told me... I'm sure you told me."

"No, we didn't," said Angus. "We haven't told you anything about them, or what we've been investigating."

"It's you!" cried Charlotte, pointing at Trevor. "You're the one behind all this."

"What, me?" Trevor looked incredulous. "No. Absolutely not."

"How else would you know that Oliver and Tom have something to worry about?" she said.

Trevor stood frozen, his mouth gaping open. Then he rallied, "Don't be silly. Why would I hire you to find out who was threatening the club if I was behind it all?"

"Because if word got out that there might be match-fixing going on, your scheme wouldn't work," said Angus. "You needed there to be no suspicion, and the only way to achieve that was to find out who was behind the threats and get rid of them." He jerked his head towards Screwball.

"Did he make you do it? Or are you the one pulling all the strings?"

"Keep your trap shut," Screwball muttered, giving Trevor an evil look.

Charlotte gasped. "That's terrible. You killed Coach Clarke!"

"No I didn't!" shouted Trevor. "It was him!" And he pointed at Screwball.

At that moment, the lights in the room came on.

"Careful, Trevor,"said Screwball, his voice low. "Think about what you're saying. The lights are on. The game can continue."

Charlotte looked out of the window. The pitch flood-lights were still off. "No chance," she said. "I've made sure my computer virus switches them off every time they come on."

Screwball stepped towards her. "You have no idea what you're getting into, love. Switch them on, or you'll regret it."

Charlotte drew herself up and faced him. "I don't think I will. I'm not scared of you."

Angus felt his phone vibrate in his pocket. He took it out. It was Simon calling him back. He put his arm out, warning Trevor and Screwball to stay back, and answered. "Simon, you need to get to Devon Rugby Stadium straight away. I'm in the executive suite. Come now. And bring help." He ended the call.

"Who was that?" Screwball asked.

"The police."

Screwball swaggered towards the door. "I'm off."

Angus moved in front of him. "No, you're not."

Screwball took another step forward until his face was centimetres from Angus's.

The stand-off lasted a few seconds before Screwball

growled and lunged at Angus. They tumbled to the floor, with Angus underneath.

Charlotte watched in horror as the two men fought. Screwball was flailing, hitting wildly. Angus fought to contain him, with some punches hitting his torso. Then Angus flipped Screwball over and onto the floor. While he was prone, Angus grabbed his arm and bent it back. "Get off, get off!" Screwball yelled.

"Get Nigel," Angus panted. "Or someone else from security. We can't let him leave while he has Rachel trapped."

Charlotte ran out of the room and down the stairs, hoping Trevor wouldn't hurt Angus while she was gone. When she got to the front desk, Nigel was there. "You have to come to the executive suite now!" she cried. "There's been a fight." Nigel stood up, his eyes round, and followed her upstairs.

When they got to the executive suite, Angus still had firm hold of Screwball, face-down on the floor.

"Wow, that hold really works," Charlotte said.

Nigel gazed at the scene before him, and Trevor stepped forward. "Stop this man from leaving," he said, pointing to Screwball.

Nigel looked from Trevor to Angus, unsure what to do.

"You'll regret this, Trevor." said Screwball, as soon as Angus let go. He stood up, brushing himself down.

"It's over," said Trevor. "I can't do this any more. You killed Lee."

Screwball eyed the three men and adjusted his shirt.

Several people from the executive box piled into the room. "Er, sorry, folks," said Trevor. "There's been a technical fault. The match has been abandoned."

Groans turned to chatter as the guests wandered out of the room.

Time seemed to stretch as Angus and Charlotte waited for the police to arrive. It was fifteen minutes by Angus's watch before Simon came in, with three other officers. "Sorry for the delay, Angus," he said. "We had to fight our way through the crowds to get here."

"You've missed most of the fun," said Charlotte.

Simon gave Angus an enquiring look.

"She's right," said Angus. But once I've explained what's been going on, you'll have the pleasure of making not one, but two arrests." He glanced at Trevor and Screwball, who flinched.

Chapter Twenty-One

The next day, Charlotte, Angus, Helena and Grigore were sitting in a row on Charlotte's Chesterfield sofa, watching the giant TV screen which had been lowered from the ceiling.

It showed the skyline of Exeter, streaming live. At the bottom of the screen was a caption: *'LIVE FROM EXETER: WW2 BOMB CONTROLLED DETONATION.'*

"How much longer?" Helena asked, looking at her watch. "Lunch ready soon."

"They said it would be 1pm," said Angus, "but I'm guessing they'll triple-check everything just in case. Better to delay than have something go wrong."

"The paperwork must be a nightmare," Charlotte, had gleeful thoughts of Angus's ex-wife Rhona at the council having to put extra hours of work in.

A voice from the screen said: "We've just been told that the controlled explosion will take place in thirty seconds."

They all stared. Exactly thirty seconds later, a cloud of

debris shot high into the air. The boom came a moment later.

Charlotte blinked. "That was more extreme than I anticipated. That isn't my idea of a controlled explosion."

Helena glanced at Angus. "Your house vill be damage."

Charlotte gazed at the screen. "From the look of it, most of the debris is going in the opposite direction to your house, Angus."

Angus didn't say anything, but the look on his face showed his concern. He wouldn't be allowed to visit his house until tomorrow morning at the earliest. It felt surreal that a bomb dropped on Exeter long ago could have such an effect now.

Helena stood up. "I get lunch ready." She smiled at Angus. "That make you feel better."

Ten minutes later, they were all sitting at the dining-room table as Helena entered with a large serving plate. "Baked fish with cream sauce," she said proudly, "and walnut bread to go vith. It my grandmother recipe."

Grigore helped himself as soon as the plate was set down and started eating. Angus helped himself to the white fish and bread. He had to admit that although it was an unusual lunch, it was delicious. The cream sauce was light, made with soured cream and a touch of paprika.

Just as they had finished eating, the doorbell rang. Helena answered it, and came back with DS Simon Pearce.

"Sorry for interrupting your meal," he said. "I came to update you on the case. Unless this is a bad time?"

"Go ahead," said Charlotte, gesturing at a spare seat next to Angus.

The officer sat down. "Trevor Holland has confessed to match-fixing," he said. "It's been going on for at least six months. He claims he had nothing to do with the coach Lee

Clarke's death. Apparently, that was down to Gavin Brooks, aka Screwball. Trevor claims that he told Screwball to stop Clarke spilling the beans about the match-fixing and Screwball killed him."

"That's awful," said Charlotte.

"It is," said Simon. "Trevor says that he didn't want Gavin to kill Clarke, just threaten him."

"Let me guess," said Angus, "Screwball has denied it."

"He did at first," Simon replied. "Then we found a large quantity of drugs in one of his gyms, hidden inside some free weights. Among them were canisters of the legal high that Clarke was given. The lab is analysing it to see if it has the same composition as that of the canister that killed him." He paused. "As a result, Screwball admitted that he did give Clarke the drug, but said that he hadn't meant to kill him. He's claiming manslaughter."

"A likely story," Helena said. "He guilty like puppy sat next to pile of doo doo."

Charlotte stifled a laugh.

"Well, that's up to the courts to decide," said Simon, managing to keep a straight face. "But Screwball's aim was to silence Clarke, so it will be up to the Crown Prosecution Service to decide whether he'll face a charge of murder or manslaughter. And now that Screwball has been arrested, his other victims are coming forward. So far, his rap sheet includes multiple threats and violence. Their criminal operation is extensive."

"Their?" said Charlotte. "Are there others?"

Simon nodded. "Screwball was one of the main gang members, but it's a complex criminal operation which will take some time to investigate fully. Even if Screwball cooperates."

"That will keep you busy, then." Charlotte popped a small piece of walnut bread in her mouth.

"What about the match-fixing?" asked Angus. "Have they admitted that?"

"Yes: Screwball admitted to forcing Lee Clarke, Tom Hunter and Oliver Miller into match-fixing. He seemed quite proud of it, in fact; he said the other gang members were impressed."

"A strange thing to be proud of," said Angus.

"It seems that instilling fear into large, muscular rugby players gave the gang kudos. At any rate, the players were frightened to come forward because the gang had threatened their family and girlfriends. The gang were known to dish out violence to anyone who crossed them."

"How did Trevor get involved, though?" asked Charlotte.

"He was unwise enough to borrow money."

"Why would he borrow money?" She frowned. "Surely he had enough of his own."

"He did, but he gambled it away. Then he took a loan out with Screwball..."

"Oh dear." Angus shook his head. "Gambling never pays."

Simon nodded, then glanced at Charlotte. "Thanks to Miss Lockwood shutting down the floodlights, Oliver and Tom's girlfriends were set free when their captors realised the game was over. Some of the gang members were at the game and reporting back to them. They've given statements about their experience, which include the detail that Screwball threatened them, and they are very relieved it's all over." Simon nodded at Angus. "Tom Hunter wishes to thank you for everything you did, Angus. He regrets the being so rude to you last week. He was being threatened by Screwball, and he was worried about his girlfriend."

"Were they aware that Trevor was behind it all?" Angus asked.

Simon shook his head. "They had no idea."

"Trevor was a lifelong Devon Rugby fan. How could he do something so awful to a club he claimed to love?" Charlotte asked.

"Zat happens ven you get in debt," Helena said. "All principles go out of vindow." She flicked her hand and made a swishing noise.

Silence fell. "Well, that's about it," Simon said, and stood up.

"Thanks for coming," said Angus, and stood up to see Simon out.

When he returned to the dining room, he was holding the local newspaper.

He sat back down. "I found this on the mat. Rather an interesting article."

Charlotte raised her head.

Angus read out the headline. "*Exeter Community Centre Comm Fab celebrates after anonymous £100,000 donation.*"

He glanced at Charlotte, and continued. "Exeter community centre Comm Fab have been celebrating after an anonymous donor gave £100,000 on their JustGiving Page.

Muriel Jones, founder of the community project, said, "At first we thought it was a mistake – you know, someone accidentally adding too many zeros – and we contacted JustGiving to check. A few days later, they told us that the donor hadn't made a mistake. I was ecstatic; I couldn't believe it. We were wondering how we'd get through the next few years, as money has been tight for so long. Now we can afford some much-needed improvements to the building and keep the community projects going."

"Aww, isn't that lovely. Someone donated to Comm Fab." A smile played on Charlotte's lips.

"That was a really kind thing to do." Angus put the paper on the table.

Charlotte gazed at him. "I was just settling that agreement I made with you."

Angus rolled his eyes. "You didn't have to donate that much! And we only got *some* info on him, not everything."

Charlotte shrugged. "It gave us a good lead and we found out eventually. It's practically the same thing. Besides, the centre does good work and helps a lot of people."

Angus eyed her. "I'll have to make a more specific arrangement with you next time."

Chapter Twenty-Two

Angus and Charlotte stood at the end of Angus's road with a council employee. He was a man in his fifties, wearing a bright yellow jacket with "*MONITOR*" on the front and back, and clutching a clipboard.

"We've assessed all the properties in the exclusion zone, and they won't fall down," he said.

"What? The damage is that bad?"

The man nodded. "There has been considerable damage to those properties nearest the bomb, and yours was close Mr Darrow."

"But it's not going to fall down?"

"No. A council representative is stationed on every road, to help you sort out repairs."

That didn't bode well. Angus's mind rushed ahead to a worst-case scenario: a shell of a house, with months of work needed.

The officer saw the anxiety on Angus's face. "Try not to worry, sir. The council will pay for any windows and doors that need replacing or repair, and from what we've seen, that's the usual damage."

He moved the barrier aside and let Angus and Charlotte through.

Angus walked up the street towards his house. At first it looked normal, but as he moved closer he saw that one of the front windowpanes was cracked. The front door was warped out of shape. The flower pots outside were broken with compost scattered on the ground.

"Shit," said Charlotte. "The other houses are the same, though. Not that that's any comfort."

Angus shifted his gaze from his house to the others nearby. They'd all suffered similar damage: windows were smashed, doors buckled. The street felt abandoned, ghost-like, and he felt huge sympathy for anyone caught in a war.

He walked up to his front door. The lock had held, but the top and bottom of the door were bent. Angus found his key, and after a couple of goes, the door opened.

He stepped inside tentatively and entered the lounge. The photo of his daughter Grace had fallen on the floor and the frame had broken, but otherwise, nothing seemed to be damaged.

He went through to the dining room and felt a cold rush of air. The patio door had been blown off and lay cracked on the tiles, its glass smashed.

"Bloody hell," Charlotte said, behind him. "There's no way you can move back until this is fixed. Stay at mine as long as you want."

"Thanks." That was the silver lining. "I'll just check upstairs."

Charlotte followed him. The spare room and bathroom showed no signs of damage, but his bedroom window was cracked and the wardrobe door had been flung open.

"Well, well, well," said Charlotte said. "I did an internet

search *and* asked my brother, and had no luck at all." She had a huge grin on her face, and Angus gave a her a puzzled look. "All I had to do was get myself into your bedroom!"

She pointed to a photo, somehow unbroken, hanging on the wall. It showed a twenty-something, smiling Angus in uniform, standing with a senior police officer and two people who Charlotte guessed were Angus's parents.

"You look very young there," she said. "The uniform suits you, just as I imagined. Was that your passing out?"

Angus joined her in front of the picture and chuckled. "Yes. It was a great day. My parents were very proud."

Charlotte turned to him. "Still don't regret leaving?"

"Still a no. Just think, I'd never have met and worked with you." He smiled at her.

"That's one of the nicest things you've ever said to me." She looped her arm through his. "Come on, let's get back to mine, and as a reward, you can pick the film to watch tonight."

A few hours later, after an Indian takeaway and a bottle of wine, Charlotte and Angus sat together on the Chesterfield, watched the film credits roll up the screen.

"What did you think?" Angus asked.

"It was good, although the technology was a bit unrealistic," said Charlotte. "I mean, hacking into the Pentagon that quickly was a joke. It would take weeks."

He nudged her. "You know that for sure?"

Charlotte smiled up at him. "I'm happy to teach you everything I know, Angus. It's never too late to change career. Once you've got used to the technology, it's actually a lot easier than you think."

"I don't want to learn how to hack, program or whatever

else it is you do," he replied. "You stick to that, and I'll remain blissfully ignorant." His face grew serious. "But it doesn't change the fact that your help was invaluable, and I'm the one who takes the fee."

"You know you can't pay me," said Charlotte. "That's against the rules of my business sale."

"You break the rules all the time."

She shrugged. "I signed a contract and I have to stick to it. I need this work. It helps me much more than anything else."

Angus looked into the distance. "I just don't understand you. A stickler for some rules, while you completely ignore others."

"I'm just full of contradictions, aren't I?" She smiled. "The therapy is worth much much more to me. Anyway, we've been over this before."

"I know, but I still don't like it."

"I love it. I get to do all sorts of interesting shenanigans with computers. Besides, who else can annoy you like I can?"

Angus stretched his arms above his head and yawned. "You've got an answer for everything, haven't you?"

Charlotte grinned. "Always."

The End.

Dear Reader,

A WW2 bomb was really discovered in Exeter in 2021. The residential area it was found in had to be evacuated and the bomb detonated. If you want to watch that, go onto YouTube and search *WW2 bomb Exeter*.

. . .

Special thanks to Sonya Ellis, Trevor Sharp, Natalie Overson, Ian Harrison and other members of the *Exeter - Past and Present* Facebook group who helped with my questions about how the real WW2 bomb discovery was handled in 2021.

Pre-order the next book in the Lockwood and Darrow Series: Exe Post Facto, book 5:

A cold case. A convicted murderer who swears he's innocent.

Lockwood and Darrow are hired by a convicted murderer to prove his innocence.

When everything points to him having committed the crime, can they find the truth?

My Book

SIGN up to my newsletter on my website to get a FREE Lockwood and Darrow short story.

www.suzybussell.com

Suzy xx

Printed in Great Britain
by Amazon

18349195R00100